Sadopaideia

SADOPAIDEIA

WORDSWORTH CLASSICS

The paper in this book is produced from pure wood pulp, without the use of chlorine or any other substance harmful to the environment. The energy used in its production consists almost entirely of hydroelectricity and heat generated from waste material, thereby conserving fossil fuels and contributing little to the greenhouse effect.

This edition published 1995 by
Wordsworth Editions Limited
Cumberland House, Crib Street
Ware, Hertfordshire SG12 9ET

ISBN 1 85326 612 4

Typeset in the UK by Antony Gray
Printed and bound in Denmark by Nørhaven

❧ ❧ ❧

Contents

VOLUME I

VOLUME II

❧❦

Sadopaideia

Volume I

The Interrupted Boston

I first met Mrs Harcourt at my College Ball, my last term at Oxford. She had come up for 'Commem' to chaperon the cousin of one of my chums. Only the blessed ceremony of marriage gave her this right, for she was still well under thirty. I learnt from Harry that she was a widow, having married an elderly and somewhat used-up brewer who most considerately died quite soon after marriage, having, I have every reason to believe, decidedly shortened his life by vain, though praise-worthy, attempts to satisfy his wife's insatiable appetite.

She was a little woman, beautifully made, with magnificent red-brown hair, the fairest possible skin, a bust that was abundant without being aggressively large, a neat waist with splendidly curved hips, and in a ball dress – discreetly yet alluringly cut – she fired my passion at once.

Harry was very *épris* with his cousin and so was only too glad for me to take Mrs Harcourt off his hands. We danced one or two dances together. She had the most delightful trick in the boston of getting her left leg in between mine now and then. At first I thought it was an accident, but it happened so repeatedly that I began to suspect, and my old man began to suggest, that more might be intended. At last I felt what seemed a deliberate pressure of her thigh against my left trouser. John Thomas responded at once, and I, looking down at my partner, caught her eye. There was no mistaking the expression. She gave a little self-conscious laugh and suggested that we should sit out the rest of the dance.

Now I had helped to superintend the sitting-out arrangement and knew where the cosiest nooks were to be found. After one or two unsuccessful attempts, when we were driven back by varying coughs or the sight of couples already installed (in one case a glimpse of white drawers showed that one couple had come to quite a good understand-ing), I succeeded in finding an unoccupied Chesterfield in a very quiet corner of the Cloisters. Here we ensconced ourselves, and without further delay I slipped my arm round my partner's back, along the top of the couch, and, bending down, kissed the bare white shoulder.

'You silly boy,' she mumured.

'Why silly?' said I, putting my other arm round her in front so that my hand rested on her left breast.

She turned towards me to answer, but before she could speak my lips met hers in a long kiss.

'That's why,' she said, with a smile, when I drew back. 'Kisses were meant for lips, it's silly to waste them on shoulders.'

I needed no further invitation. I pressed her close in my arms and, finding her lips slightly parted, ventured to explore them just a little with my tongue. To my great joy and delight her tongue met mine. My hand naturally was not idle. I stroked and squeezed her breast, outside her frock first, and then tried to slip it inside, but she would not allow that. 'You'll tumble me too much,' she murmured as she gently pushed it away. 'I can't have my frock rumpled, people would notice. Take that naughty hand away.'

As I didn't obey, she took it herself and placed it with a dainty little pat on my own leg above the knee. 'There it can't do any harm,' she added with an adorable smile. She was going to take her own hand away, but I held it tight. I drew her still closer to me and kissed her again and again, my tongue this time boldly caressing her own. She gave a little sigh and let herself sink quite freely into my arms. By this time the old proverb that 'a standing prick has no conscience' proved its truth. My right hand released hers and I took her in my arms, my right arm this time encircling her below the waist, with the hand clasping the left cheek of her bottom. Modern dresses do not allow of much underclothing and I could distinctly feel the edge of her drawers through the soft silk of her frock. 'Oh, you darling,' I murmured as I kissed her. By my taking her close to me, she naturally had to move the hand which had gently held mine. It slid up my leg and at last met John Thomas, for whom my thin evening-dress trousers proved an alto-gether inadequate disguise. She gave a little gasp and then her fingers convulsively encircled him and she squeezed him fondly.

That was enough for me, my hand slid down her frock and up again, but this time inside. It found a beautifully moulded leg ensheathed in silk, dainty lace, the smooth skin of her thigh, and at last soft curls and the most delightfully pouting lips possible to imagine. My mouth remained glued to hers, her hand grasped my eager weapon, and I was just about to slip down between her knees and consummate my delight when the lips that I was fondling pouted and contracted, and I felt my hand and fingers soaked with her love, and I realised that her imagination had proved too much for her, and that while I was still unsatisfied, she had reached at least a certain height of bliss.

She pulled herself together at once, and just as I was unbuttoning my trousers she stopped me. 'No, not here,' she said. 'It's too dangerous, and besides, it would be much too hurried and uncomfortable. Come and see me in town, there's a darling boy. Now we must go back and dance. This naughty fellow,' she added, playfully patting my trousers, 'must wait.' She then got up, arranged her dress, and, giving me a lovely kiss with her tongue, led the way back to the ballroom. I followed, but do the best I might, John Thomas took his revenge on me by weeping with disappointment, which made me extremely sticky and uncomfortable, and but for Mrs Harcourt's invitation to see her in town, my evening would have been spoilt.

❧ 2 ❧

An Afternoon Call

I 'went down' next day, and on arrival in town I lost no time in calling on Mrs Harcourt at her little house in South Molton Street. When I rang at the door, it was opened by a very neat though not particularly pretty maid, as I thought. She had, however, quite an alluring little figure and a perky naughtiness in her face which is perhaps more fascinating even than mere beauty.

'Is Mrs Harcourt at home?'

'I will see, sir, will you come this way. What name shall I say?' She showed me into a delightful little morning-room, very tastefully furnished, and disappeared. She did not keep me waiting long, but returned and said:

'Will you come this way, sir? Madame is in her boudoir. Shall I take your hat and stick?'

She took them from me and turned to hang the hat on the stand. The pegs were rather high, and in reaching up she showed the delightful line of her breast and hips and just a glimpse of a white petticoat underneath the skirt.

'Is it too high for you? Let me help,' I said.

'Thank you, sir,' she said, smiling up at me.

I took the hat over her shoulder and hung it up. She was between me and the hatstand and could not move until I did. I lowered my arm and drew her towards me. She looked up at me with a provoking smile. I bent down and kissed her lips, while my hand fondled the delightfully plump breast.

'You mustn't,' she murmured. 'What would mistress say, if she knew?'

'But she won't know,' I answered as my hand went further down to the bottom which her tight skirt made very apparent.

'She will if I tell her,' she smiled. 'You naughty boy,' and she playfully patted my trouser leg as she passed me.

'Which, of course, you won't,' I said lightly, as I followed her. She laughed rather maliciously I thought, though I didn't pay much attention at the time. I had reason later, though, to remember it.

We went upstairs and I was shown into a lovely room where a log fire was burning, although it was no colder than most June days in this country. There was a splendid deep low couch, or rather divan, for it had no back, facing the fire, covered with cushions, which took my eye at once, and I mentally promised myself what should happen on it. My expectations fell far short of the reality, as will be seen.

Mrs Harcourt was sitting on a low chair near the couch. She was in a delightfully fitting tea-gown, cut fairly low at the neck, with very loose sleeves. It clung to her figure as she rose to greet me, and being made of chiffon with a foundation of pink silk, it gave one the idea at first that she was practically naked.

'Bring up tea please, Juliette,' she said to the maid, who disappeared.

'So you have found your way here,' she said, coming towards me with outstretched hand.

The room was heavily scented with perfume, which I learnt came from burning pastilles, and she herself always used a mixture of sandalwood and attar of roses. As she approached me her perfume intoxicated me, and without saying a word I clasped her in my arms and pressed long hot kisses on her lips. To my intense delight I found she had no corsets on, and her supple body bent close to mine, so that I could feel every line of it. My hands slipped down and grasped the cheeks of her bottom as I pressed her stomach close against my trousers.

'You rough impetuous bear,' she smiled at me. 'Wait till the tea comes up.' And she disengaged herself from me, playfully slapping, as she did so, John Thomas, who was naturally quite ready by this time for anything. 'Oh, already,' she said as she felt his condition. 'I told this naughty fellow at Oxford that he would have to be patient, and he must learn to obey.'

Tea appeared most daintily served, and on the tray I noticed a delicate Bohemian-glass liqueur carafe and two liqueur glasses.

'Do you know crème de cacao?' said Mrs Harcourt. 'It's rather nice.'

She poured out tea and then filled each liqueur glass half full of the dark liqueur and poured cream on top.

'*À votre santé,*' she said, touching my glass with hers. Our fingers met and a thrill ran right through me. I drank the liqueur off at a gulp and leant towards her.

'You greedy thing,' she laughed. 'That's not the way to drink it. No, no, wait till we've had tea.'

As I tried to get her in my arms, she scolded: 'Naughty boys must not be impatient,' slapping John Thomas again and somewhat harder this time.

I sat back on the couch and drank tea rather gloomily, Mrs Harcourt watching me teasingly. At last she put her cup down and, reaching for her cigarette box, took one herself and offered me one, then leant back in her chair looking at me with a smile.

'It's a shame to tantalise him so, isn't it?' she said at last.

I did not answer, but jumped up and threw my arms round her, kneeling in front of her and covering her face and neck with kisses. She tossed her cigarette into the grate and undid the silk tie of her gown. It fell back and showed all she had on was a dainty chemise of the finest lawn and a petticoat. My right hand immediately sought her left breast, and pulling it out I kissed and sucked the dainty nipple, which responded at once to my caress, stiffening most delightfully. My left hand then reached down to the hem of her petticoat and began to raise it.

I felt her right arm round my waist and her left hand began to unbutton my fly from the top. Before she had time to undo the last button John Thomas leapt forth ready and eager, but she slapped him and pushed him in again, undid the last button and fumbled for my balls, gently drawing them out. I drew back a little from her and lifted her petticoat right up, disclosing the daintiest of black silk openwork stockings with pale green satin garters, and above them filmy lawn drawers with beautiful lace and insertion, through which the fair satin skin of her thighs gleamed most provokingly. At the top there appeared just between the opening of the drawers the most fascinating brown curls imaginable.

I feasted my eyes on this lovely sight, undoing my braces and dipping my trousers down. Her hand immediately left my balls and began to fondle my bottom, stroking and pinching the cheeks while she murmured, 'You darling boy, oh, what a lovely bottom.'

I was eager to be in her, but the brown curls fascinated me so much that I could not resist the temptation to stoop down and kiss them. I was rather shy of doing this, as I had never done it before, and though I knew it was usual with tarts, I was not sure if it would be welcome here. Judge of my surprise, then, when I felt Mrs Harcourt's hand on my head gently pressing it down and heard her saying, 'How did you guess I wanted that?'

She opened her legs wider, disclosing the most adorable pussy, with pouting lips just slightly opening and showing the bright coral inner lips, which seemed to ask for my kisses. I buried my head in the soft curls, and with eager tongue explored every part of her mossy grot. She squirmed and wriggled with pleasure, opening her legs quite wide and twisting them round me. I followed all her movements, backing away on my knees as she slipped off the chair, until at last, when she drenched my lips with love, she lay partly on the hearth rug. Then, as I could scarcely reach her with my tongue in that position, and didn't wish to lose a drop of the maddening juice, I disengaged her legs and knelt down to one side so that my head could dive right between her legs. This naturally presented my naked bottom and thighs to her gaze.

'You rude naughty boy,' she said, smacking me gently, 'to show me this bare bottom. I'm shocked at you.'

Her hands again fondled my balls and bottom, and I had all I could do to prevent John Thomas from showing conclusively what he had in store for her.

I had no intention of wasting good material, however, and was just about to change my position so that I could arrive at the desired summit of joy when I felt her trying to pull my right leg towards her. I let myself go and she eventually succeeded in lifting it right over, so that I was straddling right across her, and we were in the position I knew quite well from photographs, known as sixty-nine.

My heart beat high. Was it possible I was to experience this supreme pleasure of which I had heard so much? I buried my head between her thighs, my tongue redoubled its efforts, searching out every corner and nook it could find, and just as it was rewarded by another flow of warm life I felt round my own weapon, not the fondling of her hand, but something softer, more clinging, and then unmistakably the tip of a velvet tongue from the top right down to the balls and back again, and then I felt the lips close round it and the gentle nip of teeth. This was too much, John Thomas could restrain himself no longer, and as I seized her bottom with both hands and sucked the whole of her pussy into my mouth, he spurted forth with convulsive jerks his hidden treasure. When the spasm was over I collapsed limply on her, my lips still draining her life.

❧ 3 ☙

An Afternoon Call – continued

I was aroused quite soon by her pushing me off her chest. 'Get up,' she said, 'you are crushing me.' We both got up and stood for a moment looking at each other. Then she felt for her handkerchief and wiped her lips. I tried to take her in my arms.

To my surprise she pushed me away. 'Go away,' she said, 'I don't like you.'

'Why, what's the matter?' I asked.

'Matter!' she replied, and she seemed to be working herself up into a temper. 'Matter! You horrid beastly boy, how dare you come in my mouth?'

'I'm sorry,' I said, 'it happened so quickly and I – I – I thought you wanted it.'

'Wanted it! How dare you?'

I tried again to put my arms round her, but she wouldn't allow it.

'No, get away, pull your trousers up and go.' And she turned to ring the bell.

I sprang to her. 'Don't send me away,' I said. 'I'm sorry and I won't do it again. Forgive me. Let me stay a little and forgive me.'

'Let you stay?' she laughed. 'What's the use of your staying? Look at yourself.'

And she pointed to poor John Thomas, very limp and drained dry and looking very ashamed of himself.

'Oh, he'll be all right again in a little time,' I said. 'Come, darling, let me stay and show you how much I love you,' and I managed to get one arm round her and draw her to me. She let me kiss her but kept her lips quite shut, so that I couldn't get my tongue into her mouth. Her body was quite stiff, instead of yielding as before. I grew bolder and caressed her breast and began to pull up her petticoat again. She seemed to take no notice for a minute or so, and then, just as I had uncovered her thighs and was feeling for the soft curls of her mount, she quietly pushed my hand away, detached herself from my arms, and said quite calmly, 'Well, if I let you stay, you must be punished for your rudeness. Will you do exactly as I tell you and submit to any punishment I may inflict?'

Now I knew nothing at that time of flagellation. I had heard of old men needing the birch to excite them, but beyond that I knew nothing. So I said, 'Punish me in any way you like, only let me stay and prove to you how sorry I am and how I love you.'

'Very well,' she said, 'get behind that screen,' pointing to a large Chinese screen that stood in the corner. I obeyed and she rang the bell.

Juliette appeared. 'Take the tea things away and bring me my leather case.'

I thought I heard a chuckle from Juliette but was not sure. After a little while I heard her come in again and whisper something to her mistress. 'Yes, very,' replied the latter. Then came more whisperings and I heard Mrs Harcourt say, 'Oh, did he? Well, we shall see.'

She then told me to come out, and I obeyed. I must have made rather a ridiculous figure, as my trousers were still down. Mrs Harcourt, however, did not seem to show any disposition to laugh. In fact, she looked very angry indeed. I went towards her, but she stopped me with a gesture and said, 'You promise to do everything I tell you.'

'Anything,' I said.

'Very well. Turn your back to me and put your hands behind you.'

I obeyed.

She opened the case and took something out, I could not see what, and then she came to me. I felt something cold touch my wrists and heard a snap. I tried to move my arms and to my surprise I found I could not. She had, in a moment, very deftly handcuffed me. I was too surprised to speak. 'Now kneel down,' she said.

'What for?' said I.

'You promised to do everything I told you,' she repeated.

I knelt down awkwardly enough, with my hands fastened behind, just in front of the big couch. Then Mrs Harcourt took a large handkerchief and blindfolded me. I didn't like the look of things at all, but said nothing.

'Now,' said Mrs Harcourt to me as I knelt there helpless, 'you have been a very rude and dirty boy and you must be punished. Are you sorry?'

I was just about to answer when 'whish', something whistled through the air and I felt as if a hundred needles were pricking my bottom. I could not help an involuntary cry.

I heard a sigh of pleasure, and felt a hand on my neck, pressing me forward on to the couch.

'Are you sorry, eh?' she repeated, and again came the smart cut across my bottom.

I had never been birched in my life. At school a tanning cane was used, but I could easily guess what was the weapon she was using.

'Will you speak? Are you sorry?' she repeated, and again the rod descended. I tried to escape but my hands' being tied hampered me, and though I could and did kick lustily, her hand on my neck managed to prevent me escaping altogether.

'Keep still,' she said, 'or I shall get Juliette to help me. Are you sorry?' At that moment in one of my struggles the birch just caught my balls, causing excruciating pain.

'Yes, oh yes,' I shouted.

'Will you ever do it again?' – whish – whish.

'No.'

'What was it you did? Confess your fault.'

Silence on my part. I felt too angry and ashamed to say.

'Will you confess?' – whish – whish – whish.

'Oh yes, I will.'

'Well, what was it?'

'I came in your mouth.'

'And what else?' – whish – 'what else?'

'I don't know.'

'Didn't you say you thought I wanted it?'

'Yes.'

'Well, confess then.'

'I said I thought you wanted it.'

'Ah!' and again the blows fell all over my bottom.

The burning pain got worse and I struggled and wriggled and kicked so that I at last got away from her, managed to rub the handkerchief away from my eyes and swung round and looked at her.

I never saw such a change in any woman. If she was pretty before, she was lovely now. Her eyes were shining, her cheeks were flushed, the exertion of plying the rod had caused one shoulder strap of her chemise to break and one breast was just exposed.

I looked at her with adoring eyes. I couldn't help it. Angry and hurt as I was in my dignity and elsewhere, I could not but feel admiration and – yes, even affection. She met my eyes.

'Well,' she said, 'why have you turned round? I haven't finished yet.'

'Isn't that enough?' I said. 'I've said I'm sorry and confessed my fault.'

'Haven't you any other faults to confess?'

'No!'

She rang the bell.

I exclaimed, 'You're surely not going to let anyone see me like this?'

She made no reply and the door opened and Juliette appeared.

'Juliette, come here,' she said. 'You see this gentleman here; now repeat before him the accusation you whispered to me just now.'

Juliette looked at me with a malicious smile (I remembered that smile) and said, 'When I was hanging the gentleman's hat up in the hall, he offered to help me, and then he kissed me and felt my breast and tried to feel my pussy through my skirt.'

'You little cat,' I said.

'Is that true?' said Mrs Harcourt. 'Answer me,' and the birch fell across my thighs as I lay twisted on the couch. It flicked up my shirt-tail and exposed John Thomas to the salacious gaze of Juliette. I was too ashamed to speak.

'Will you answer me!' and again and again came the cutting strokes, one of them just catching poor John Thomas nicely.

'Well, if I did, she did as much to me,' I muttered.

'Oh, indeed,' said Mrs Harcourt, as Juliette darted a vicious look at me. 'Well, we can investigate that later. Get the bands, Juliette.'

Juliette went to the case and produced a long band of webbing-working on a loop and, before I knew what she was about, had slipped it round my ankles and drawn it tight. Now I was indeed helpless.

'Now Juliette,' said her mistress, 'as it was you who were insulted, it is only fair for you to punish him.'

They turned me over face downwards and turned up my shirt.

'Oh, he's had some already, I see,' said the maid.

'Yes, a little,' said the mistress. 'He can do with some more.'

'How many,' said Juliette, taking up the birch.

'We'll see.'

Then the pain began again. Blow after blow, cut after cut, until my poor bottom felt as if it was on fire. I wriggled as much as I could but couldn't do much. My motions, however, must have pleased Mrs Harcourt, for she said, 'Wait a moment, Juliette, we mustn't be too hard. He shall have some pleasure as well as pain.'

She got round to the other side of the couch, raised my head, which was buried in the cushions, and, bending down, whispered to me, 'He's a naughty boy, but I love him, so he can kiss me if he likes.'

She then pulled up her clothes and presented her pussy backwards to me which I could just reach with my tongue.

'Now Juliette,' she said, 'not too hard, and cleverly.' I did not feel at all anxious to justify her wishes, but to my surprise the birch fell now in quite a different way. Instead of the slashing cuts which had made me writhe and smart, the blows simply warmed my bottom. Of course now and then it touched an extra sore place and made me flinch, but for the most part the twigs seemed to caress, and the tips of them, curling in between the cheeks, gave me a delightful sensation, and I felt John Thomas answering in a way that surprised me. I forgot my resentment against Mrs Harcourt and my tongue roamed about her lovely pussy and even went higher and caressed the other 'fair demesnes that there adjacent lay' and which presented themselves to my eyes, a proceeding which evidently pleased her, for she opened and shut the cheeks of her bottom, and at last with a quick side twist and a final plunge she forced her pussy right against my mouth, and murmuring, 'That will do Juliette,' she smothered my mouth and chin with her delicious cream.

She then got up and with Juliette's aid undid my bonds. I lay still, too excited to move. I felt her arm round my neck, while her other caressed my bottom. 'Poor boy,' she said, 'did it hurt very much?'

I turned round and kissed her. I couldn't help it. All my rage and feeling of insult seemed to have disappeared. 'That's right,' she said, nestling close to me. 'So the whipping did him good! It didn't go on too long though, I hope,' she added, quickly pulling up my shirt and looking at my John Thomas, who by this time, after the last part of the birching, was nearly bursting. 'No, that's all right. Come to me, darling.'

'But Juliette!' I said.

'Oh, never mind her ... Still, perhaps she had better go,' she added with a peculiar look. 'Juliette, you can go, I shall want you in a quarter of an hour.

Juliette looked very disappointed, but had to go.

'Now, darling,' said her mistress, 'come to me and love me, and say you forgive your cruel mistress for hurting you.'

She unfastened the band of her petticoat and let it fall. Then she stepped out of it. Her teagown was wide open, and, as I have said, one shoulder of her chemise had broken, so she was practically naked to the waist.

She went to the chair again and sat down right on the edge, lying right back so that her bottom jutted just over the edge. I knelt before her and found her pussy was just at the right height for John Thomas.

Her legs went over my shoulders and I gently placed him in position and began work.

I have never known such an expert in the art of love. Every conceivable motion and twist of her body she used. Her eyes flickered with passion, her lips drew my tongue right into her mouth, while her hands led mine all over her body. She murmured words of love and desire, mingled with pity for my poor bottom. At last she said, 'He was a very naughty boy, but it was a shame to cut him up so badly. Never mind, someday perhaps he will have a chance to retaliate.' Then the final paroxysm came on and we were both dumb. My motions, which had been slow at first, grew quicker. She plunged and writhed, twisting her legs round my neck and raising her bottom to meet my strokes, until at last, with a half-sob, half-groan, her legs fell down from my shoulders and I poured into her eager womb a deluge of my love.

❧ 4 ❧

An Afternoon Call – continued

We remained motionless like that for a few moments, our lips glued together, our bodies held close to each other. Then Muriel said, 'Now I'd better ring for Juliette and towels and water.'

We got up and she pressed the bell. Juliette appeared. It was too late now for any modesty on my part. Juliette had seen all I had to show her, so what was the use of pretence. 'Hot water, towels and soap, Juliette,' said her mistress. The maid turned to go. 'Oh, yes, and some special cream for the poor bottom,' she added with a smile.

Juliette disappeared and her mistress turned to me and said, 'Let's look at the poor little bottie. Turn round, is it much cut up? Look for yourself.' She led me to a mirror fixed down on the wall. I looked over my shoulder. Certainly my poor bottom showed distinct marks of the birch. The skin had not been actually cut, but there were red and violet marks interlaced criss-cross all over it. Also, it was very tender to the touch.

'Poor boy, what a shame,' said Muriel. 'Still, it will do him good and teach him not to be naughty again.'

I smiled a little ruefully. But she flung her arms round my neck and said, 'Oh, I love you, darling, every bit of you, and I love your poor dear bottom most of all.'

Juliette entered at this moment with a tray on which were a sponge, a silver rose-bowl, some soap and towels, and a pot of cream.

She put them on the table and her mistress turned to me.

'Juliette will wash you,' she said. Juliette approached me. 'Will you stand here, sir, please,' she said, pointing near the table.

I did so. She took John Thomas in one hand and held the bowl in the other. Then she plunged him into the water, gently drawing the foreskin back while she gently rubbed the glans with her fingers. Then she put the bowl down and, taking the soap, soaped him well and sponged him thoroughly, washing all the bush and between my legs. Then she took the towel and thoroughly dried all the parts. 'Turn round, please.' I turned round. She lifted my shirt and performed a similar service to my bottom. Finally she took some of the cream and rubbed it on the tender places. A delicious cool feeling came over me and all the smarting disappeared. She then raised my trousers, buttoned them, and turned to her mistress.

'Madame is ready?'

'One moment, Juliette,' said the latter. 'Just now you accused Mr Prendergast of taking liberties with you and you punished him for it.'

'Yes, madame,' said Juliette.

'What was it you said he did?'

'He kissed me and felt my breast and tried to feel my pussy.'

'Quite so. Now Mr Prendergast did not deny that but he said something in reply. What was it?' Juliette turned pale. 'Answer me.' Still no reply. Muriel turned to me. 'What was it you said?' she asked.

'Oh, it doesn't matter,' I said, for now the pain of the whipping had passed away I did not feel revengeful. 'Never mind what I said.'

'But it does matter and I do mind. If I'm not mistaken you said she did as much to you. Am I right?'

I looked at Juliette. She gave me a frightened look.

'Muriel, dear,' I said, 'never mind that, forget it.'

'Oh, I'll forget it in due time,' she answered. 'Now, Juliette, answer me. What did you do? You know you had better speak the truth . . . When Mr Prendergast kissed you, did you kiss him back?'

'Yes,' in a whisper.

'Did you do anything else?'

Juliette glanced at me. 'I just patted his leg and said he was a naughty boy.'

'Oh, and what part of his trouser leg did you pat? Show me?' Juliette timidly patted me again. 'I thought so,' said Muriel sternly. 'I guessed as much. So you complained to me that Mr Prendergast kissed you and tried to feel your pussy, though you at the same time kissed him and tried to feel what he had. Well, you have punished him for his rudeness. Isn't it only fair that you should be punished too?'

I interposed. 'No, Muriel, it was my fault, I began it.'

'I'm glad you realise that, Cecil, it shows that your whipping did you some good. But I must be the judge of what is proper behaviour in my servants. There was no need for her to imitate you. Now Juliette, don't you think as Mr Prendergast has been punished, it is only fair that you should be so too? Eh?'

'Yes, madame,' said the poor girl.

'You see you have only yourself to blame,' went on Muriel. 'If you had not told me what Mr Prendergast had done, I should have known nothing about it and you would have escaped. Now get ready.'

'What, before Mr Prendergast?' stammered Juliette.

'Of course, he was punished in front of you, in fact by you, so it's only fair that he should have a share in your punishment.'

The tears rose to Juliette's eyes as she began to undo her belt. The skirt slipped off to the floor. The petticoat followed it. She stepped out of them and stood in her chemise and drawers with downcast and blushing cheeks.

Muriel went to the case and took out a fresh birch. 'Go to the couch. Kneel down.'

Juliette started and then rushed to me and, flinging herself at my feet, sobbed out, 'Oh, sir, I'm so sorry I told on you. Don't let her whip me. I'm sorry I whipped you.'

I felt awkward. I was not naturally cruel and I did not bear the girl any grudge. At the same time I felt a keen desire to see her naked bottom and to see her wriggle under the birch.

I lifted her up and said I would do my best to persuade her mistress.

The latter was growing impatient. I went to her and begged her to let the girl off lightly. She laughed and said, 'All right, I'll stop when you tell me to.'

I then led Juliette, still weeping, to the couch. She knelt on the edge of it and buried her face in the cushions.

'Lift up your chemise and open your drawers,' ordered her mistress. She did as she was told, disclosing two white globes of which no lady need have been ashamed. A dark shadow just between them gave promise of a beautiful dark forest in front. As she was kneeling on the couch and not on the floor as I was, her bottom was raised higher than her head and the skin stretched quite tight.

'Now,' said her mistress, 'I'll teach you to tell tales of my guests when you yourself are equally guilty,' and whish–whish–whish came the birch on the plump cheeks. Juliette sobbed and cried and nervously contracted her bottom to meet the strokes. 'There, there, there, and there,' went on her mistress, 'will you kiss visitors in my hall again, and try and pat their privates? Will you, will you?' The blows descended in quick succession, now on one cheek, now on the other.

Juliette bounded up and down, but did not, as I did, kick about. She knew better. At last two cuts more vigorous than the others and rather lower down were too much for her and in desperation she had to move her legs.

'Ah,' said Muriel exultantly, and quick as lightning she rained a shower of blows in between the thighs, reaching with the ends of the twigs the pouting lips of the pussy that Juliette's struggles disclosed.

Juliette shrieked and, letting her body collapse, tried to cover her poor bottom with her hands.

Muriel looked at me. Till then, for the life of me, I could not have interposed to stop the whipping, but now I managed to stammer, 'That will do,' and Muriel dropped the birch and fell into my arms.

John Thomas had grown greatly excited by the scene, and taking no thought of Juliette, who lay moaning and twisting on the couch, I pushed Muriel on her back beside her and mounted her. Our course was quicker than might have been expected, seeing that I had already done my duty twice that afternoon. I suppose the excitement of seeing Juliette birched and the heating effect of being birched myself had a great deal to do with it. Anyhow, Muriel and I both swam together in a perfect sea of bliss before many moments had passed.

Juliette, perceiving that her whipping was over and that other things were happening, sat up beside us and began to dry her eyes with her chemise.

Her mistress, noticing this, said, 'Well, I'm afraid you can't feel Mr Prendergast's affair now, Juliette, it's too busy; but he can feel your pussy quite well,' and she took my hand and pushed it towards Juliette's thighs.

The latter did not dare to resist and I soon found the secret grotto I wanted, and, pushing my fingers well in, gave her some slight gratification in return for her whipping.

When we had finished and had got up, Muriel said, 'You will have to wash Mr Prendergast again.'

'May I do it my own way?' said Juliette.

'If you like,' said her mistress, 'but I don't expect you'll get any good from it.'

To my surprise Juliette knelt down before me and began licking and sucking my limp weapon, but though John Thomas wept a little, I had done too much that afternoon to be able to give any real performance, and after a while she gave it up as a bad job and began to dress herself.

Muriel laughed and I felt a little ashamed, but I promised myself that before long Juliette should have a taste of my quality in more senses than one.

'Come again soon,' said Muriel, as she kissed me goodbye most lovingly, and I promised I would without fail.

As Juliette was showing me out, I said, 'Well, if I kiss you now, will you tell your mistress?'

Her only answer was to put up her lips, and when my lips met hers she pushed her tongue right in my mouth while her hand clutched my old man convulsively.

'*You* tell her *I've* kissed *you*,' she murmured, 'and then she will make you whip me yourself. I'd love to be whipped by you. I'd suck and kiss you while you were doing it till you dropped the birch with faintness.'

Before I could reply she had opened the door and I found myself in the street.

◆§ 5 §◆

An Inopportune Arrival

When I reached home I tried to analyse my feelings and realise what had happened. I could barely believe it was true. It seemed like an impossible dream. Here was I, just down from Oxford, aged twenty-three, submitting to be whipped like a naughty boy on my bare bottom by a woman whom I had only met once, and in the presence of another girl whom I had never seen before I called on her mistress. More than that, I had poked and 'kissed' the mistress and had been 'kissed' by both mistress and maid. Still more, neither woman was a whore in the usually accepted sense of the word. The one was accepted as chaperon for the cousin of my best pal and evidently mixed in quite good society. The maid to all appearance was eminently respectable. No. I couldn't believe my own experience. It was only when I sat down to think things out that my sore bottom brought the truth palpably home to me. I jumped up with a cry and rushed upstairs to my bedroom, locked the door, and in a twinkling had my trousers down and was investigating my bottom in the looking-glass. Gad! but I was marked. Long lines of purple and red showed criss-cross all over both cheeks, with here and there a spot of bright red where the buds on the birch had broken the skin. I got some ointment which I used for soreness after rowing and gave myself a liberal dose. Then I washed John Thomas, who was looking thoroughly ashamed of himself, dressed myself and went downstairs.

My feelings were difficult to analyse. Shame, anger, and a wish for revenge fought with each other. At the same time Muriel's charms were ever before me, and at moments John Thomas made gallant attempts to persuade me that the afternoon was worth everything. Juliette's bottom also rose before my eyes white and plump and round, quivering under the blows of the birch, opening and shutting between the strokes and showing glimpses of the dark pouting lips of her pussy – that pussy which I had felt and found so responsive to my fingers.

What were her last words? 'I should love *you* to whip me.' By Gad, I thought, why not? Surely it was worth risking another whipping myself to get the chance of making those lovely cheeks flinch and squirm. And then Muriel! What a gorgeous poke. How her tongue had caressed my old man. How her pussy had drawn every bit of life from me! Yes, undoubtedly I must call again.

So I argued that night. But next morning doubt and nervousness came over me again, and eventually it was quite a week before I rang the bell again at the little house in South Molton Street.

Juliette opened the door and smiled when she saw me. 'Madame was wondering why you had not called,' she said. 'She is rather angry with you, sir, in consequence, I fancy,' she added with a meaning look. 'She does not like to be neglected. But she is not at home now.'

'Can I come in and wait?'

'Oh, yes, sir, if you like.'

So I went in and shut the door. She led me into the little morning-room and for a moment we looked at each other. Then without any delay or explanation, we seemed to fall into each other's arms, our tongues met, and our right hands dived straight between each other's legs. John Thomas rose at once and I found Juliette's soft little pussy already dribbling with expectation. I urged her gently back to an armchair and, kneeling before her, placed John Thomas in the haven where he would be. Her bottom lifted itself to meet him and we came together in a mutual flood of love.

'Tell me, Juliette,' I said when we had finished, 'does Muriel whip you often?'

'As often as she gets the chance,' she said with a wry little smile.

'But why do you submit,' I said, 'and how did it begin? It isn't usual for maids to be whipped.'

'I'll tell you someday,' she answered. 'It's too long a story for now. Besides, she's very good to me and I get more pleasure with her than I should anywhere else.'

She cuddled close to me and fondled John Thomas, who evidently enjoyed it.

'You said something to me as I was going away last time that puzzled me,' I said after a minute.

She blushed a little.

'Come,' I said, 'do you really like being whipped?'

'Don't you?'

'No, I'm damned if I do,' I answered with a laugh.

'Oh, you will in time. I don't always. There are different sorts of whippings. I didn't like being whipped the other day by Muriel in front of you, for she was wicked and jealous. But you, when I whipped you, didn't you like it? Wasn't it different to the whipping Muriel had given you?'

'Yes,' I said reflectively, 'it certainly was different.'

'Well,' she went on, 'if I like a person I *do* like him or her and want to do all and everything to please. With Muriel, for instance, when she's nice and wants me' – she blushed a little as she said this – 'I'm willing to submit to anything. I know she wants to see my nakedness and watch my bottom wriggle, so I do all I can to gratify her, but when she's angry and only wants to punish me, I hate her and want to hurt her.'

'Haven't *you* ever whipped her?'

'Good Lord no! That's not her game, she's no Masochist. I only wish she were and I had the chance. I'd pay her back. But she's much too strong for me, and besides, I'm different, I don't like giving pain and she does. It's only when I'm angry with her.'

'Hm,' I said.

'What are you thinking of?'

'I was thinking, well, I don't know much about this matter, but I know this. I'd love to get my own back for my last call here. Now you and I together, eh? Couldn't we master her?'

Her eyes gleamed, then dropped. 'She'd kill me,' she said.

'Oh no. I'd see she did not do that. I'd make her promise to bear no malice and I don't think she would. If she did, I'd see you came out all right. The worst she could do would be to turn you out, and then you could come to me. I am looking for a flat to settle down in and should want a housekeeper, eh?'

'Oh, that would be lovely,' she replied.

'But you haven't answered my question. Would you really like *me* to whip you?'

'Try,' was all she answered. And before I knew what she was doing she had slipped off the chair and pulled up her skirt and petticoat above her waist behind, showing her dainty drawers.

'Sit down there,' she said, pointing to the chair she had just left.

I obeyed her. She then laid herself across my knees, face downwards with her head towards my left arm, and pulled her drawers open behind, showing the beautiful curves of her bottom, the cheeks of which stood out like two lovely white moons, though still slightly marked from last week's whipping.

'Now smack me and see if I like it.'

I gazed at the snowy globes with the shady valley between. Just at the meeting of her legs a few tendrils of dark hair showed themselves, promising other, more secret delights.

I smacked her lightly with my hand. It was more of a caress than a blow.

She lay still.

Smack–smack–smack, and my fingers crept between her legs.

'No, not yet,' she said, 'I want you to smack me.'

I humoured her and I smacked both cheeks quickly till they began to grow pink.

'Harder, harder!'

I smacked more severely. Her bottom became appreciably warmer.

'Harder still,' she said, 'harder!'

I did as she said, and my own hand began to tingle. The joy and lust of domination began to grow in me.

After one or two really hard blows, she shifted slightly and heaved her bottom, opening her legs a little.

I gave her several harder smacks. She sighed and wriggled. I stopped.

'Go on,' she said at once.

'But I'm hurting you.'

'I want you to hurt me,' she murmured fiercely. 'I want you to hurt my bottom. Can't you see it growing red and hot? Hurt me, hurt me.'

Her passion, though I didn't really understand it, fired me, and I took her at her word. Blow after blow fell on her plump cheeks and at length her sighs came quicker and quicker and became more like gasps. Her bottom heaved and opened and contracted, her legs parted and I could see the lips of her pussy parting and closing again as if eager for satisfaction.

Desire now took full possession of me and I smacked her as hard as I could, seizing every opportunity of making my hand reach the more hidden and secret retreats. It was a strange and maddening delight to me. After two or three blows on her firm bottom I felt my fingers strike the softer lips of her pussy. Once or twice I managed to reach that delightful spot with my finger tips while my palm just managed to get between the plump cheeks. This seemed to madden her as much as it did me. She flung her legs apart, pushing up her bottom, keeping it as wide open as possible. She muttered inarticulate cries, and at last after several blows which hit both marks full, she sank down heavily on my knees, imprisoning my hand between her thighs, which closed on my fingers like a vice. I felt her pussy throb and throb again and then a warm flood spread all over my hand.

I raised her up and held her close in my arms. 'You darling,' she murmured, 'take me, I am yours utterly.'

Her hands slid down and with feverish haste unbuttoned my trousers.

John Thomas, as was only to be expected, was rampant.

'Give him to me,' she half-sobbed.

'How would you like him?' I asked with interest, for I had not forgotten how she had asked to be allowed to wash it in her own way.

'Any way, so long as he is in me . . . in front, behind, any way, I don't care. I'm yours, all of me. Take all of me, darling, my master!' and she threw herself at my feet, embracing my legs, half-sobbing and writhing with unappeased passion.

I lifted her up to her knees and she seized my affair with her lips and, flinging her arms round my bottom, began to lick and suck it with avidity.

'Oh, so that's the way you entertain my guests in my absence, is it?' I turned hastily. There stood Muriel. She had evidently just come in. Her latchkey was still in her hand. She was holding the door open.

❧ 6 ❧

The Tables are Turned

Juliette collapsed on the floor with a cry of terror. I stood stock-still like a fool. Certainly I must have presented a ridiculous figure, trousers unbuttoned, a rampant engine well exposed.

'Get up, you,' said Muriel to Juliette, going to her and touching her with her foot. 'You,' turning to me, 'can either go or stay, but if you stay . . .' She paused ominously.

'I'll stay,' I said, for I had an idea.

'As you please. I see I have arrived in time,' looking at my open trousers. 'So you can . . . but . . . I rather think you will be sorry.'

She led the way upstairs, and I found myself again in the boudoir.

Juliette was already there, shaking with nervousness. 'Where are the cases?' thundered Muriel at her. 'Did you think I had you up here to talk to you?' and she suddenly gave her two swinging boxes on the ears.

The poor girl hurried out of the room.

'Muriel,' I urged, 'don't be too cruel to her. It was my fault chiefly.'

'Don't you fret yourself, my man, *you'll* get all *you* want.'

Juliette reappeared carrying the leather case which I recognised.

'Both cases, you fool,' said her mistress.

Juliette gave an even more terrified cry than before, but did not dare to argue.

She went out and came back with another, similar case.

Muriel unlocked the first. 'Undress yourself,' she said; then to me: 'And you tie her hands with this,' giving me a long piece of webbing. 'I must take my corsets off or I shan't have freedom enough for my arm.'

Juliette tremblingly undid her skirt and let it fall, and waited.

'Everything,' said her mistress, 'didn't you hear? Everything, or it will be the worse for you.' Juliette then undid her blouse and took it off. A dainty camisole appeared. That was removed. Then the petticoat. Then the little corsets were undone and she stood simply in chemise and drawers, the lace frills of the latter peeping alluringly below the hem of the chemise. Her trembling hands groped under the chemise, she pulled the string and the frilly little legs fell round her ankles. She stepped out of them and stood waiting.

'I thought I said everything!'

A crimson flood invaded the poor girl's cheeks and neck.

'You needn't pretend to such modesty sneered Muriel. 'A girl who will kneel down to kiss a man in a sitting-room needn't be shy of stripping naked before him in a boudoir, especially when there is another woman to protect her.'

Juliette lifted the chemise and began to pull it over her head. I saw first her thighs appear, beautifully shaped and moulded like towers of ivory, then the dainty little bush, still dewy with our mingled love; next a sweet rounded little belly, smooth and firm. I noticed the dainty waist line and, above, two perfect pear-shaped breasts with bright red nipples standing out firm and bold, though all support had been removed. As she raised her arms above her head, I saw the silky hair in her armpits, matching the thicker curls of her bush.

Then the chemise slipped off her wrists and she stood, a slight timid figure, perfect, desirable and appealing.

I heard a sigh of appreciation from Muriel. 'Now tie her wrists together,' she said to me.

I had to obey. She watched me as I fumbled with the webbing.

'Now stretch her on the couch.'

I bent her down as she had been bent down the other afternoon.

'No, not that way. She must be crucified.'

'Madame,' stammered Juliette.

'Silence,' hissed Muriel as she placed some cushions across the middle of the couch, forming a ridge.

She then dragged Juliette to the couch and flung her face downwards so that the lower part of her belly and the top of her thighs rested right on the cushions. This naturally raised her bottom and thighs, making her body form a very broad inverted V.

'But what's the meaning of this?' she said as she saw the cheeks of the poor bottom still blushing slightly from my recent smacking. 'Do you mean to say you've dared?' she went on, turning to me. 'Oh, you just wait.'

She said no more but took hold of Juliette's right ankle and pulled the leg towards the edge of the couch. Then, stooping down, she caught hold of a silk cord that was fixed to the side of the couch, evidently for that purpose. It had a running loop at the end. This she slipped over the girl's foot and drew it tight. She then pulled the other leg as far apart as possible and fixed that in the same way.

Poor Juliette was now perfectly spread-eagled. Her arms were above her head tied at the wrists, her head was buried in the couch. Her bottom was raised, as I have said, by the ridge of cushions and seemed to invite the lash, and her wide-opened thighs revealed the mossy lips of her pussy, still slightly open. There she lay, a piteous little figure, all white.

The only contrast was her dark hair, slight silky tendrils in her armpits, the suggestive shadow between the cheeks of her bottom, the soft curls between her legs, and last of all, showing up vividly against the whiteness of her skin, her long black silk stockings, just a study in black and white, no touch of colour anywhere, for she wore black garters. I feasted my eyes on the lovely vision. How could anyone, I wondered, hurt such a dainty graceful creature?

I looked at Muriel. Her eyes showed clearly that she was by no means insensible to the alluring picture. But there was a gleam of fierceness as well as admiration in her glance.

'Now,' she said suddenly, 'I must get rid of my corsets. I shan't be long. You can admire the dainty darling's white skin while I'm gone. There won't be much white left after I've finished with her,' and she went quickly into her bedroom, leaving the door open.

Now, I had decided to stay in the hopes of carrying out my scheme of vengeance on Muriel, and I had no intention of assisting at the punishment of Juliette. But when I saw the preparations and how helpless Juliette was rendered by her bonds, I began to doubt the possibility of succeeding in my object. Though no doubt I could have mastered Muriel by brute strength, there would probably have been a struggle, and Juliette's help would have been of the greatest use. All the time Muriel was pinioning Juliette my mind was working quickly, but I hesitated to make any attempt to seize her, preferring to wait until the last moment.

Now, however, that she was out of the way I saw my chance. Quick as thought I sprang to Juliette's wrists and began to loosen the knots. She raised her head, gave a little cry of surprise and fear. I put one hand on her mouth and whispered, 'Keep quiet and pretend to be still tied. Remember what I said downstairs. Now is our chance. Keep your hands just as they are, till I tell you. Then free your feet and help me.'

I had only just time to loosen the knots and replace the webbing so that it still looked tight, and to get away from the couch, when Muriel appeared. She had put on the tea-gown again, with the loose sleeves. I was standing by the table when she came in, looking at the open case which contained the birches. There were four different sizes.

'Looking at my little ticklers?' she smiled. 'There are some more in here,' and she opened the other case.

Then I understood Juliette's cry of alarm when Muriel told her that she wanted both cases.

There were no birches in this one. Two or three canes of varying thicknesses, a couple of old-fashioned ladies' riding whips – not the modern hunting crop, but whips of long flexible whalebone with lashes at the end – a whip of seven knotted cords, very fine, but looking very wicked, and last of all a sort of birch made of wire, the ends of which were bent at right angles.

'Pretty, aren't they?' said Muriel, laughing. 'They'll come in later. We'll begin with this.'

She turned to the other case and selected a long pliant birch, weighing it in her hand and swishing it in the air.

Now was my opportunity. As she turned from me to the couch and the prone girl waiting, I suddenly flung my arms around her, pinioning both arms tightly to her side.

❧ 7 ❧

The Fascination Begins

She was completely taken by surprise. She had scarcely time to gasp out an exclamation of anger. 'Juliette,' I cried as she struggled violently in my arms.

Juliette quickly got her wrists free and, reaching down, got her ankles from the loops. Then she ran to me as I was holding the squirming, kicking Muriel.

The latter was like an eel. She kicked, she bit, or tried to, but my arms were tight round her middle, and as she had taken off her corsets, my grip crushed her ribs and gradually winded her.

Juliette, avoiding with difficulty the kicking legs, managed to get the band of webbing round first one wrist and then the other and draw it tight. My grip had not relaxed and in a comparatively short time Madame Muriel's wrists were bound together.

She still grasped the birch and all the time was pouring out indignant and angry expostulations. There was no trace of fear, however, as yet. Pride, rage and hate showed in every glance and tone.

When Juliette had finally and satisfactorily tied her hands, I dragged Muriel to the couch and pushed her on to it. She sat and glared at me, out of breath and exhausted.

Her tea-gown had come unfastened at the waist and fell apart. Except for her stockings and shoes, she was absolutely naked. She evidently had intended to have a perfect field day. Well, she should not be disappointed.

I turned to Juliette with a smile: 'Well, what shall we do to her? How shall we begin? You know more about these things than I do.'

'Spank her first; the hand will prepare her bottom nicely for the birch,' said she. 'Shall I hold her down for you?'

'No,' I said, 'I'll hold her and you can begin. Come along, Muriel dear. This is a little different from what you intended, isn't it? It will be a new experience for you, eh? Will you turn over of your own accord or shall I help you?'

She made no answer, so I went to her and took her by the wrists. She dragged her hands away and suddenly, bending down, seized one of my hands with her teeth and bit it hard.

'You little devil,' I shouted, 'you shall pay for that,' and I brought my other hand heavily down on her ear and cheek. The force of the blow knocked her head on one side and made her release my hand. With a quick twist I turned her over and held her face-down on the couch, her legs hanging over the side. Juliette stood at one side of her and, dodging the kicking, plunging legs, proceeded to deliver a shower of smart smacks on the plump cheeks and thighs.

The blows fell at random, here, there, and everywhere, with no direction and without much real effect, as Muriel was dodging too much. After a minute or so Juliette stopped and looked at her palm.

'It's hurting me more than her,' she laughed; 'we'd better begin seriously. Put her as she put me.'

I pulled Muriel further on to the couch and managed to get her belly and thighs over the ridge of cushions; I then leant heavily on her back, while Juliette with great difficulty secured one leg in the silk loop.

All this time Muriel was struggling and shouting: 'I won't be tied down, I won't be whipped. Don't you dare to touch me, or I'll pay you for this afterwards.'

I took no notice, but when her legs were firmly secured, I pulled the tea-gown up over her shoulders as far as I could and said, 'Yes, it's a little different to what you intended, isn't it? Instead of you feasting your eyes on our naked bodies and enjoying the sight of our bottoms reddening and writhing under your blows, it's *your* nakedness we are going to look at, it's *your* bottom and thighs that are going to blush and quiver. Are you looking forward to the treat? Come, answer me.'

'I'll kill you,' she hissed.

'Oh, no you won't, you're going to beg my pardon, to beg both our pardons, in fact, and thank us for showing you your proper place. Now Juliette, will you begin? I'll enjoy the scene for the moment.'

I kept my left hand pressed on her back and with my right I stroked the beautiful loins and bottom and thighs, which lay bare to my touch. If Juliette had made an alluring picture with her dark hair and clear white skin, her mistress easily rivalled her. She was a little the plumper of the two and fairer, and whereas Juliette's colouring was pale, Muriel's skin was flushed slightly with pink. Their two bodies made a delightful contrast.

The idea struck me of comparing them, and when Juliette came back with a birch I asked her to lie beside her mistress for a moment so that I might see both their naked bodies together. She obeyed at once, and I revelled in the lovely vision. So lovely was it that I could not resist the temptation but took out my old man and was about to make good use of the favourable position of the two girls. But when Juliette saw what I was about, she stopped me.

'That will come later; business first,' and she got up and stood by the couch, raising the birch in the air.

'Now madame,' she said, 'just a little gentle correction for your impudent bottom. How do you like it?' as the twigs fell right across the left cheek. 'You are so generous with it to others, you ought to be grateful. Is it nice? nice, eh? nice – nice? . . . Oh, you're sulky, are you, you won't speak, won't you, we'll see about that. Answer me at once, will you? at once – at once.' The blows fell quicker and quicker, but Muriel made no sound. She lay practically motionless with her head buried in the couch. Her flesh flinched each time the blows fell across her bottom, but she made no cry or any sound.

'Still obstinate,' said Juliette; 'we won't allow that and must per–severe.' She came round to the other side and proceeded to visit the other cheek. Then she went lower and cut across the thighs, but though Muriel's contortions grew more convulsive, she still kept silent, until at last one blow of the birch curled right between her legs and a stifled cry of pain escaped her lips.

'Ah, I thought I should succeed before long,' said Juliette, as she rested for a moment. 'Will you begin now, sir?'

I took the birch, or what was left of it, for the twigs had broken off at every stroke.

What a change now in Muriel's bottom. No longer was the skin clear and pink and white. An angry red flush covered the centre of both cheeks, from which ran lines of red and violet which disappeared round the legs and cheeks towards the hips.

'Now Muriel,' I said, 'Juliette has finished for the moment. It is my turn now. I am going to give you a lesson in behaviour towards your guests. How do you like that, and that,' as the swift strokes fell. 'Will you answer me?' I went on, as she still remained dumb, and the blows redoubled.

'There!' said Juliette, pointing with her finger between the cheeks of Muriel's bottom and the legs stretched wide open. 'That will make her speak.'

I followed her advice and gave three crashing blows that cut and curled along the inside of her thighs and reached the hidden lips of her pussy.

They evidently proved effective. Shriek after shriek came from Muriel as she twisted and writhed.

'Not there, let me go,' she cried. 'Oh, oh, oh. No, don't, don't, no more,' as the blows fell again.

Hysterical sobs shook her whole body. I stopped whipping her and said, 'Ah, you've found your voice have you? Well, are you going to behave better in the future?'

'Oh, yes, yes!'

'And do you like being whipped,' I went on, 'and is it as nice as whipping others? Do you like showing your nakedness and your bottom to Juliette and me?'

She only sobbed in reply and I thought she was punished enough and was going to release her when Juliette saw my intention and stopped me.

'No, no, not yet, she hasn't had nearly enough. Don't you remember, she said I was to be crucified? Well, I know what that means; I've had some.' She went to the other case and brought out the two riding whips and a couple of canes and gave me one of each. I dropped the stump of the birch and waited.

'Now madame,' she said, 'you've shown me more than once what you call crucifixion. I hope I shan't forget your teaching. Let me see. This comes first, doesn't it?' and she brought the cane heavily across both cheeks of the quivering bottom.

A shriek of pain from Muriel. She raised herself up and twisted herself to one side to avoid the blow. I had left her when I had finished birching her, so that she could move freely, except that her hands and feet were tied.

'By Jove, that seems to touch the spot,' I said, 'how do you like that, dear? It seems a little more effective than the birch. What does it feel like? Come, tell me.'

Muriel only groaned and writhed convulsively.

'Come, answer me, or can't you quite tell from one cut? Does that make it clearer to you?' and I brought the cane heavily down about half an inch below the livid weal left from Juliette's blow.

A positive howl of anguish came from Muriel.

She raised her body and twisted about as if she was on fire.

'You mustn't move about like that. Not only are you making a most indecent exhibition of yourself but you are doing no good. Come, what is it like? Is it nicer than the birch or do you miss the tingling twigs?'

Still no reply, but sobs and moans. I grew impatient. 'Will you answer?' and I made the cane whistle through the air, but didn't touch her with it. Her bottom shuddered with apprehension.

'Oh, it's awful,' she gasped, 'it's like a bar of hot iron burning into my flesh.'

'Ah, well, you're going to have quite a lot of those hot bars. In fact, your bottom will be quite a gridiron before we've finished with it.'

'Yes, but she mustn't plunge about like that,' said Juliette, 'or we shan't be able to get a pretty pattern on her bottom and thighs. She likes pretty patterns, I know, for she has often shown me the designs she has traced on me after she has finished. There's nothing like neatness and finish for any work. If a thing is worth doing, it's worth doing well. That's what you often say, isn't it, madame?' she sneered.

Muriel didn't answer.

'Ah, she's lost her voice; we'll find it for her in a minute. Will you help me, sir?' She seized her mistress's wrists: 'There should be a cord here. As you say, sir, there is no use in countenancing any more indecent exposure than is necessary.'

She found a cord at the head of the couch similar to those that fastened Muriel's ankles. She fastened it to the webbing round the wrists and drew it tight. Then she took up the cane again and went back to her former position.

'Will you, please, stand opposite me, sir, and take your time from me? Don't hurry and be careful how you place your blows. There should be room for a dozen a side, I should think.'

She measured carefully with her fingers the distance from the dimples just above the cheeks, where the plumpness began to swell, down along the thighs to just above the knees.

'Yes, she can take twelve easily, I fancy. Will you try to keep an accurate distance between each cut just as you have already?'

She pointed to the two livid blue marks, which contrasted with the untouched skin between them.

'Now,' she said, raising the cane and bringing it down just below the dimples at the top of the checks. An angry red line appeared and another shriek from Muriel.

I raised my cane. 'Just there,' said Juliette, pointing just below.

Crash fell the cane. Another yell.

'What, more hot iron?' sneered Juliette.

Crash fell her cane just below my mark and crash my cane followed hers.

'Don't hurry,' she insisted. 'We've only got a dozen each. It will do none of us any good; she won't be able to appreciate each separate cut and we shall be finished before we have begun. It would be a pity for her not to realise the care we are taking to do the thing properly.'

'Shall we count the strokes out loud, then we shall be more deliberate,' I said.

'Let her count them to us,' said Juliette. 'Let me see, that makes four. Four, do you hear, madame? Now please call the others.'

I took hold of her hair and raised her head. 'Do as you're told. That was four. Count the rest. What comes next?'

I pulled her head right back. 'Five,' she gasped in terror.

'Five it is,' said Juliette, and again the cane fell.

'Oh, mercy, mercy,' moaned the victim.

'Go on counting.'

'Six.'

I let go of her hair and, carefully directing the cane, brought it down just below Juliette's last mark.

We had just reached the summit of the rounded hillocks and the cane fell full on the firm flesh.

'Ah, God,' said Muriel, 'I shall die, you are killing me.'

'I'm not dead,' said Juliette, 'and I've had more than this from you, and I haven't got so much fat to protect me as this,' she added bitterly, rubbing her hand down over the wounded flesh. Muriel shrank under the touch. 'Well, we are waiting, madame. Hadn't you better continue? The sooner it's over, the better for you.'

'Seven,' gasped Muriel, and the seventh blow fell.

'Eight.' I followed. 'Nine. Oh, finish, finish, for pity's sake.'

'Now, you're too impatient! Is it so nice that you can't wait? Well, there you are then, as you seem to want it.'

'Ten, eleven, twelve.' The blows had now reached the thighs, softer and more tender than the plumper cheeks. The cane gave quite a different sound and a still more piercing shriek came from Muriel. She tried with all her strength to drag her feet from the loops and bring her thighs together. But the cords held firm and she could only contract the muscles of her thighs, which rose and fell again on the ridge of pillows. Her hands clutched convulsively at the webbing and relaxed. Her head rolled from side to side. Her whole body heaved.

'Perhaps we may as well finish by ourselves,' said Juliette, who seemed to be growing excited. I must admit that I myself felt a growing impatience. I wanted to strike and strike again at this helpless flesh, and my next three blows were rather at random.

'Steady,' said Juliette, 'don't spoil the gridiron.

'That's better, twenty-two, twenty-three, twenty-four.'

'There, look, it could not be better, one could write music on those clefs.'

She stood resting on the cane, panting slightly.

Muriel had stopped shrieking; only moans and hoarse choking sobs came, shaking her whole body.

I looked at Juliette. To tell the truth I was rather frightened lest we had done too much. I must have shown this in my face, for she laughed. 'Oh, don't be afraid, we haven't half-finished yet, she can bear lots more. But we must shift her for the finale. Isn't it a lovely picture, though?' and she traced the straight lines with her fingers in a fierce joy.

'Ah, madame, do you remember the first time you crucified me? I haven't forgotten. How you laughed! It's my turn to laugh now, isn't it? You didn't think then that Juliette was to have the chance to write her name on your naked bottom, or you mightn't have been so keen on showing me how it was done.'

She went to the loops which fastened the legs and took them off. 'Now turn her over on her back,' she said to me. 'Perhaps she would rather display her breasts and belly than her hinder parts.' I went to Muriel and pulled her towards me. She made no resistance. Her eyes were closed, her cheeks were wet with her tears, her whole body shook with gasping sobs. I rolled her over on her back and Juliette quickly refastened the legs. When she felt her bottom resting on the cushions, she started and screamed with the pain and tried to turn over again, but she was too late. Juliette had secured the ankles.

'Now, madame, for the real crucifixion.' She pulled open the tea-gown at the neck and displayed all her mistress's charms.

There she lay, outstretched for sacrifice, her breasts standing out firm, her belly raised by the ridge of cushions on which her bottom rested, while her legs, stretched as wide apart as possible, showed all her sex.

Scarcely a mark of her chastisement showed from our present point of view, only between her legs a few marks of the birch showed and the lips of her pussy seemed swollen slightly and flushed.

She presented altogether a maddening spectacle to my eyes, which wandered over all her body. Her position was ideal for any form of attack and I couldn't resist the temptation of putting my hand between her legs and investigating the gaping lips of her pussy.

Juliette watched me jealously. 'Do you want to be in her? I should wait till tomorrow, but you can go on doing that if you like while I finish the crucifixion. It won't interfere with me. In fact, it will make it all the more amusing. She will have two different kinds of tickling at the same time.'

My fingers began to probe the soft clinging lips of Muriel's pussy, while Juliette flicked the nipples of her breasts with the lash of one of the riding whips. She stood at the head of the couch and Muriel's white body lay stretched between us. Under the gentle persuasion of my fingers Muriel's sobs and groans gradually changed into sighs. Her thighs contracted, little twitchings and spasms ran over her smooth belly, evidently the pain of the whipping had not taken all sexual feeling from her.

'Tell me when she comes,' said Juliette eagerly, as the little lash flicked here and there with a sort of wicked caress.

'Now,' I said as I felt the lips of Muriel's pussy contract, and her bottom heaved with convulsive thrusts and her thighs contracted and imprisoned my hand.

I was not prepared for what followed. Without a word of warning, Juliette lifted the whip above her head and brought it heavily down on her mistress's body, straight up and down between her breasts, causing a long straight weal starting from the valley between her breasts, crossing the navel, and ending just above the dainty brown curls of the bush, where the lash cut the skin and a few beads of blood appeared.

Muriel's sighs and moans of passion changed to a shriek of agony, but Juliette paid no heed. She stepped to one side and again brought the whip down on the unprotected body, but this time across from side to side, just across the breasts. Another weal appeared, making a perfect cross. I felt Muriel's body grow suddenly limp. I looked at her face; it was deadly pale. She had fainted.

How beautiful she looked there, with her arms tied above her head, her eyes closed, her mouth partly open, her head drooping, the purple lines of the cross showing up on her deathly pale skin, her firm plump legs stretched this way and that, revealing the beautiful mossy curls and soft lips of her pussy, still dewy with the involuntary sacrifice to love. I looked to Juliette to see what she would do and went to unfasten the loops.

'Oh, she'll come round all right,' said Juliette, 'you needn't worry. I've had lots worse from her than that. Don't untie her yet.'

'I won't have her whipped any more,' I said. 'We've given her quite enough. Get some water and bring her round.'

Juliette went to the bedroom, and I chafed Muriel's hands and cheeks. Her eyes slowly opened and she looked at me. I was prepared for anger and resentment, but instead of that I only saw submission and appeal.

'Cruel, cruel,' she murmured. 'How could you be so cruel?'

I bent down and kissed her lips. 'I'm sorry,' I answered, 'but you had to learn who was master. Have you learnt it?'

Her eyes said yes and I kissed her again.

Juliette came back with smelling-salts and cold water.

Her mistress's eyes glowered as she saw her approach. I saw the look. 'Now there must be no resentment against Juliette,' I said. 'Let her help you to bed and take care of you, and I will call and see you tomorrow.'

'No, don't let her come near me,' said Muriel; 'I won't have her. *You* take care of me,' turning to me, 'I want *you*.'

'You will do as you are told,' I said firmly, for I realised it was the only way to keep my new-found sovereignty. 'Now Juliette, kiss your mistress and be friends.'

'Let me help you, madame,' said Juliette; 'you know I have always let you help me when you have whipped me.'

'We will both see to you,' I said. 'Juliette, get the bath ready.'

I undid Muriel's bonds and gently raised her up. She could not bear to sit on her poor bottom, but hung round my neck and across my knees, the picture of abject submission.

'Oh, my lover, my king,' she murmured, 'you have won me, you have mastered me. I am your slave, I love, I worship you.'

Juliette came back to say that the bath was ready, and between us we carried Muriel into the bathroom, which led off her bedroom, and laid her in it.

Juliette took the soap bowl and, making a lovely lather, prepared to cover her mistress with it. Some of the soap splashed on me.

'You'll get your clothes spoiled,' she said; 'you had better take them off.'

I did as she suggested and in a minute or two was as naked as they were. We soaped Muriel all over and then Juliette produced a flask of some sweet-scented oil which she gently applied to the poor scourged bottom and thighs. She dried her tenderly and laid her on the cool sheet.

Muriel gave a little sigh of fatigue and closed her eyes. I took a towel and began to dry myself. Juliette was putting things straight, going here and there quickly as she replaced bottles and soap and brushes.

It might have been Ancient Rome – Rome of the Empire. This marble bathroom, myself a young patrician, and Juliette a slave-girl attending on my wants.

I watched her slim form everywhere, my desire growing hotter and hotter, until at last she stooped down with her back to me to pick something up from the floor and in so doing showed me all her lovely bottom and the darling little pussy pouting out between her thighs.

I did not say a word, but silently came behind her, caught her round the hips and thrust John Thomas between the lips which were ready and eager to receive him.

She gave a little start of surprise, then a pleased laugh. 'You silly impetuous boy. Why not wait until we can be comfortable?'

But I was far too eager to wait and began working in and out with vigour.

'Cecil,' called Muriel, 'where are you? I want you.'

'I can't come for the moment, I'm busy. I'll be with you in a minute.'

'But I want you now. What are you doing?'

Juliette chuckled. I made no answer, but went on working. I was just finished when I saw Muriel's reflection in the glass standing on the floor.

'I thought as much,' she said.

I had finished my work and turned to face her. Juliette also turned coolly and faced her mistress.

I could not help comparing this interruption with the other, earlier on that afternoon.

'What are you doing here?' I said. 'Go back to bed. Do you want another whipping?'

'I wanted *you*,' she said humbly.

'Well, I was busy, as you see. I'll come to you in a minute, in fact, we will both come.'

She darted a look of hatred at Juliette.

'None of that,' I said, 'I won't have it. You must be friends with Juliette. Go and kiss her at once.'

She hesitated.

'Go and kiss her at once, or shall I fetch the whip?'

'Oh, no, no,' she shuddered and went slowly towards Juliette.

An idea struck me. 'Kneel down,' I said, 'and kiss those other lips of hers. You said you wanted me. Well, you'll find some of me there. Kiss her and thank her for whipping you.'

It was lovely to see the conflict of pride and fear in Muriel. She gave Juliette and me a quick glance and then, sobbing, knelt down before her maid's naked body and pressed her lips on the thick curls.

'Say what I told you to say,' I urged.

'Thank you, Juliette,' she sobbed stammeringly, 'for whipping me.'

It was too much for her and she bowed her head and wept.

Juliette's pity was moved. 'Oh, Muriel,' she said, as she gently raised her mistress, 'don't be angry with me, forgive me if I hurt you.'

She raised her to her feet and the two women fell into each other's arms.

'That's right,' I said, 'now we will go to bed.'

•❧ 8 ❧•

The Turning Point

Looking back on my life, I date my conversion – as an evangelical person would express it – from that afternoon. Until I met Muriel I had really no knowledge or experience of the vagaries of vice. My life, till then, had been absolutely normal. Apart from the usual pseudosodomy of a public school – *masturbatio intra nates*, as Krafft-Ebing styles it – which practice I discarded and despised on going up to Oxford, I had simply sought women for straightforward fornication. Naturally certain subtleties of pleasure had been learnt, but until I had suffered at Muriel's hands and had been able to retaliate, I knew nothing of the intense, though recondite, delights of domination and humiliation. I realise on careful introspection that I had always a natural bias towards sadism. Even as a small boy I played the game of 'school' with my little sister, with the natural consequence of 'whippings'. I remember also, when on a holiday in Derbyshire at the age of fifteen, finding a book in the rooms where we were staying, in which there was a whipping chapter. The orphan daughter of a poor curate became a 'town apprentice' to the wife of the local doctor. Her mistress ill-treated her and one day, finding her sweethearting with some man, gave her what was called a 'workhouse supper'. The description of this thrashing with a strap at night on the bare bottom gave me, I remember, a terrific erection, and in spite of relieving myself in the usual way of a boy of fifteen, I had that night my first wet dream when the scene of the story was vividly re-enacted in my sleep.

Anyhow, whether naturally disposed that way or not, I went home that afternoon triumphant and elated. I had achieved my object of getting even with Muriel and had, at any rate for the time being, subdued and dominated her, and the joy of possession was far surpassed by the gloating satisfaction I felt at the thought that she was my slave, subdued and humiliated.

My desire towards her for the future was no longer sexual inter-course but domination, subjection.

In this spirit I hastened to see her the next day. Before leaving her I had given her strict instructions that she was on no account to retaliate either in deed or even attitude towards Juliette for the humiliation and crucifixion of that afternoon. I had also told Juliette that if Muriel attempted anything of the kind she was to tell me at once, and that for her own sake she was on no account to submit, or it might be the worse for her. 'I am going to be your master,' I said, 'just as I am going to be hers, and I will have no one sharing my power.'

Determined therefore to keep my new-won servants, I arrived at the house next day. Juliette as usual opened the door. She was rather pale and her eyes were slightly red. I asked her what was the matter. 'Muriel has been cruel to me,' she said.

'But I thought I told you you were not to submit.'

'I couldn't help it. She has been my tyrant too long, one cannot break one's bonds in a minute.'

'What did she do? She couldn't have done much. She was too exhausted.'

'Oh, she slept after you left, but during the evening she woke up and sent for me. I found her much recovered, though still stiff and sore. She at once went for me for betraying her into your power and vowed that even though she might not be able to get even with *you*, *I* should pay for my treachery. I told her what you had said, and how you had ordered me not to submit, but she would not listen. I resisted all I knew, but she is very strong, much stronger than I, and you don't know, you can't know, what it means to have been in a woman's thrall for years as I have been. Luckily her experience of the afternoon had shaken her so much that she fainted before she had done much, but look!' She lifted her skirt behind, bent down, and pulled open her drawers. There were about a dozen livid weals right across her bottom.

'What did she do that with?' I asked.

'With the riding whip. She was going to use the wire birch, she threatened me, but the excitement and exertion of this was too much and she fainted.'

'She shall pay for it,' I said. 'But you – I told you you were not to submit to her. How dared you disobey me?'

'I'm sorry, I couldn't help it.'

'Sorry! Couldn't help it! Yes, you will be sorry and you'll learn to help it. Take me to her.'

She looked frightened at my words, but led the way upstairs to Muriel's room.

Muriel was in bed, looking rather pale but very lovely. Her hair was loose about her shoulders. She looked up as I came in and smiled with pleasure.

'Oh, Cecil, I was hoping you would come. I am longing for you.'

'Hm,' I said, 'are you? What is this Juliette has been telling me? I thought I told you you were not to retaliate for your punishment of yesterday and now I find her with a bruised bottom and she says that but for fainting you would have done more.'

'Surely I can punish my own property? I know I am your slave, but surely in my own house I am mistress.'

'*Your* property, *you* mistress? You may have been before yesterday, but now, I have learned what power means and – thanks always to you, you must remember – you are both *my* property, you obey me. If I give you permission you may perhaps be allowed to correct Juliette, but not without my permission, nor in my absence. Do you clearly understand that? Juliette, go and get the cases. I had better fix this new system in both your minds.'

Juliette obeyed. Muriel turned white and began to sob. 'You are not going to whip me again, surely. I'm sore all over still from yesterday, you could not be so cruel.'

'Oh, there must be lots of places left. Let me see.' And I pulled back the bedclothes quickly before she had time to see what I was doing.

Her nightdress had worked up and she was naked from the waist down. 'Ah . . . well, the bottom and thighs certainly are fairly marked, but the back and calves are untouched. Turn over. Yes, I thought so. Why, there's lots of room.'

Juliette returned at this moment, carrying the two cases. Muriel hastily tried to cover herself.

'Oh, modest, are you?' I laughed. 'A little late, isn't it? Now Juliette, I have been telling Muriel what I think about her conduct to you, and she will have to pay for it. But you have been disobedient, too, and must be punished. You said you would love to be whipped by me. Well, your wishes shall be gratified. You had better undress, not altogether though, or you may shock Muriel's modesty. Stay a moment, I have an idea which will prevent any false shame on her part. Give me that webbing.'

I took the webbing and tied Muriel's left ankle to her left wrist and her right ankle to her right wrist and then rolled her on her back.

She submitted as if in a stupor.

'There now, she can't see you, Juliette, and no matter how much she may gather you are exposed by the sound of my strokes, she must realise that she is far more indecently exposed herself. Besides, she will be in a most convenient position for punishment. Now go on undressing yourself.'

Juliette looked a little frightened, but at the same time there was a look of expectancy in her eyes, which gloated over Muriel's nakedness. I took a birch and all the time Juliette was undressing, I was tickling Muriel's pussy, which was stretched open owing to her position, with the tips of the twigs.

When Juliette had taken everything but her chemise and drawers off, I stopped her. 'That will do for the present. Turn the chemise up over your hips.'

She obeyed. 'Now bend down here,' pointing to a spot at such a distance from the bed that her face would just reach Muriel's bottom and pussy as she lay spread-eagled on the side of the bed, 'and put your hands on your knees. Now,' said I, 'I am first going to tan you as we did at school. Listen, Muriel, and think how you will like it when your turn comes. You can lie patiently there for the present.'

I exchanged the birch for a cane, and swinging it back with a full sweep of my arm, I brought it down with full force across the half-open drawers. The force and surprise of the blow drew a cry from Juliette and impelled her forward, so that her face knocked against Muriel's bush. The latter uttered a cry of alarm.

'What's the matter?' I asked.

'I didn't know Juliette was so close. It startled me.'

'Oh, she's quite close. She can see all you've got to show, can't you Juliette?'

'Yes, sir.'

'Well, tell us what you can see. Listen, Muriel.'

'I can see Muriel's bottom and her belly and her . . . her . . . ' She stopped.

'Her what?' I insisted. 'Her pussy?'

'Yes . . . '

'Well, tell her so.'

'I don't like to.'

'Oh, don't you. Does that make you want to?' and I gave her a vicious cut with the cane.

'Don't, oh, don't.'

'Well, say it.'

'Muriel, I can see your pussy . . . '

'Inside and out?' I asked.

'Yes, inside and out.'

'There, Muriel, you hear that? What is the good of pretending to be so modest when you are showing your pussy, even the inside of it, to your maid and me. Why, we can see right inside you. We can see your clitoris there' – and I touched it with the tip of the cane – 'we can nearly see your womb, I expect.'

'Oh, untie me, and let me go. Whip me if you want to, but don't keep me tied up like this.'

'Oh, you shall be whipped right enough, don't you worry. There's plenty of time. Still, if you're impatient we'll lay in now; move aside, Juliette. Now look out.'

I lifted the cane, made it whistle in the air. I saw Muriel contract the muscles of her thighs and buttocks to meet the blow and, to tantalise her, brought the blow down about two inches from her body. She gave an involuntary cry.

'What's the matter?'

'I thought the cane was coming. I heard it whiz in the air.'

'Oh, disappointed, are you? Well, things are always nicer when you get them when you don't expect them.'

A vicious cut of the cane pointed the 'expect' and Muriel shrieked with surprise.

I turned to Juliette, who was still bending down.

'Now, to go on with you. How many have I given you?'

'Two.'

'Two. Ah, that leaves two more. We were only allowed to give four at school.'

Whack, whack came the cane, and with each blow Juliette's face was buried in Muriel's mossy curls.

'Now take your drawers off. We will see what the cane has done. Lie on your back beside Muriel in a similar position to her.'

There were four clear red lines across the white cheeks, in spite of the protecting drawers.

I looked at the two distended bottoms conspicuously displayed on the edge of the bed. They looked so quaint that an idea struck me.

I went to the dressing-table and found a pair of hairbrushes.

Then I sat on the bed between the two girls and began to play, as it were, the side drums on their bottoms. I kept time to a mad silly sort of rhyme, something like this:

> 'Mu–riel, Mu–riel,
> I will tan your bo–ttom well.
> Ju–liét–te, Ju–liét–te,
> I will see you don't forget,'

accentuating the alternate syllables with blows of the brushes, using alternately the backs and bristles of the brushes.

I varied the force of the blows also so that they never knew what the next blow was going to be like. I brushed the hair on their pussies, now softly so that they wiggled under the lascivious caress, now fiercely as if I was scrubbing a brick, which made them squirm with agony.

Getting tired of this I again addressed myself to Muriel.

'You asked me just now to untie you and whip you, didn't you? Well, I'm not so sure that I won't do as you ask. The position is a little tiring I expect.'

'It's awful . . . My legs and arms are gone to sleep. Oh, please untie me.'

'Juliette, you may untie her, if you like. Now go and stand in that corner with your face to the wall and wait until I am ready. Don't dare to look round. Juliette, take off her nightdress and your own chemise and drawers. That's right, now go and stand beside her.'

I took a birch from the case and the whip of knotted cords.

'Now,' I said, 'I am going to whip you both for disobedience. I ordered you, Muriel, not to attempt to retaliate on Juliette for your whipping of yesterday, and I told you, Juliette, that you were not to submit to her if she tried it on. So both of you deserve and will get this,' and I brought the birch down heavily across their bottoms, one after the other. Juliette only flinched, but Muriel's bottom was so sore that she involuntarily placed her hands on her burning cheeks.

'Take those hands away,' I said, cutting them again and again. 'If you don't I will tie you down . . . Now, will either of you disobey me again?' Whish – whish came the birch across Juliette's thighs.

'Oh, no – no – never,' she sobbed.

'Will *you*,' to Muriel as I stepped across and laid the birch across her loins and calves, which were comparatively untouched. She sobbed and shook her head. 'Answer me.'

'No, oh, don't whip me so low down,' as the birch caught her on the back of her knees.

'Oh, don't you worry, you shall have enough higher up in a minute or two. Now, Juliette, I'll finish you off. Come here, kneel down facing me.'

I got her head between my thighs and laid into her with the birch right up and down both thighs and cheeks of her bottom. Occasionally I directed a blow right between the cheeks, so that the tips of the twigs curled right into her pussy. She screamed and writhed and plunged, imploring mercy.

'Do you hear that, Muriel,' I said. 'That's nothing to what you will get in a minute. Perhaps you are getting impatient, eh? Well, there's something to go on with.'

I could just reach her with the birch and let her have one cut and then came back to Juliette, whom I had kept tightly pressed between my knees. My blows had caused all her bottom and thighs to flush a dark red, on which the weals from Muriel's riding whip and my own tanning stood out across in darker colours. 'There's quite a pretty lattice work across your behind, Juliette dear. I didn't know I was such an expert at designing. Have you had enough? Do you think you will be disobedient again? Well, we will just make sure.' And I delivered a regular hail of blows everywhere as quickly as I could, until I was out of breath. Juliette's cries increased. She wriggled and twisted this way and that, but the relentless rod found her every time. Blood began to show here and there where the skin had been broken and even began to trickle down her legs. The birch twigs flew all over the room and at last I had only the mere stump left in my hand.

Then I relaxed the pressure of my thighs and she fell forward on the floor, twisting and groaning and her hands instinctively going to her lacerated bottom to protect it from further assaults.

All this time Muriel had been standing as I told her, with her face to the wall, a picture of apprehension. She knew she was within reach of my arm and so did not dare to move or look round.

I turned to her. 'Now, Muriel, come here. It's your turn.' She turned and came towards me with appealing looks. 'Go down on your hands and knees,' I ordered, 'and pick up those broken twigs. We can't have the room in this state. The sooner you finish the job, the better for you.' I threw away the birch and took up the knotted whip with the five lashes and to start her gave her a moderately hard blow on her flanks. She gasped and went down as I had told her, hastily picking up the bits of twigs here and there. It was a most fascinating sight in its shameless nakedness and humiliation. She crawled and grovelled all over the floor, trying to avoid my blows and at the same time to pick up the twigs as quickly as possible. I pursued her everywhere, taking care at first to avoid the parts still sore from yesterday's whipping. All across her back and flanks the lashes fell. Now they curled over her shoulder or cut into her armpits. The tender flesh below her ribs received many, the knotted ends reaching round to her stomach. Livid weals began to appear and at last she flung herself at my feet, her hands full of twigs, imploring my pardon and protesting that she would never disobey me again. She even begged Juliette to plead for her to me. I allowed myself to be persuaded, and told them to see to each other's comforts, but warned both of them that if ever I found them disobedient again there would be worse punishment in store for them.

I then prepared to leave them, for though the whippings had excited me, I had no desire, as I had the day before, for any actual sexual enjoyment.

'You are not going, Cecil, are you?' pleaded Muriel. 'Surely now you have punished both of us, you will be kind and give us what we want,' and she came close to me and, like a suppliant, looked imploring into my eyes. Juliette also sent appealing glances at me.

I pretended to misunderstand her.

'Haven't you been whipped enough?' I asked.

'Oh, yes, but I want – I want – '

'What?'

'Well, if I must say it, I want you in me,' she blushed and stammered.

'No,' I said sternly, 'you don't deserve it and I'm not going to satisfy your lusts. Still, you can both, as a favour, kneel down and kiss the God Priapus, whom you worship, but nothing more.'

I undid my trousers and let loose the object of their adoration and let them both approach one after the other. To humiliate Muriel, I told Juliette to come first, which she did on her knees. I did not allow her to stay too long, but made her give place to Muriel. She knelt eagerly before me and, embracing me round the hips, kissed and licked the rampant head. Human nature was too strong, and I deluged her face and neck with spurting jets of my strength. But I had no pleasure from this, as compared with the delight I had experienced while flogging their subjugated bodies.

❧ 9 ❧

I Settle My Kingdom – Juliette's Story

If I date my 'conversion' from the previous day, I may quite well look on this afternoon as my 'confirmation'. Until then I had been a man with just ordinary desires. Now physical union with a woman became quite a secondary consideration with me. The fascination of domination held me, and though, of course, I had both Muriel and Juliette as my mistresses, that was more for their pleasure than my own. For myself I was their *master*, they were my *slaves*.

I quickly settled my kingdom, and as a first proof of my position, I demanded and obtained a latchkey. With this I was able to make surprise visits, but I will say this for Muriel, she gave me no cause for jealousy. She was quite content, for the time being at any rate, with me, and although she admitted that it was quite a surprise to her to find herself submitting to any man, still she loved me for mastering her – or so she said. With Juliette, however, she was quite different. She did not exactly bear malice, but she evidently meant to get her own back. She was, however, quite aware that I would not tolerate any sly vengeance; I had made that quite clear to her; but I could see that she meant, at the first opportunity, to pay Juliette out. Nor had she any intention of giving up the autocratic sway she had wielded for many years. She put this quite frankly to me one evening. 'It's all very well for you, Cecil,' she said; 'you have mastered me – much to my surprise, I admit – still, you *have* mastered me, and I love you for it. But with Juliette, it's different. I've always had her as a subject; when we were at school together she fagged for me, and I used to whip her if I wasn't satisfied with her.'

'At school together?' I repeated.

'Yes, didn't you know?'

'No, Juliette said she would tell me someday how your domination of her began – that was that afternoon you caught us in the morning-room and got caught yourself,' I added maliciously. 'But she said it was too long a story to tell then.'

'Well, shall we have her in and tell you now?'

'If you like.'

She rang the bell, and Juliette came in. 'Juliette, Cecil says you promised to tell him how we got to know each other. Sit down and do so now.' She was sitting on my knee with her arm round my neck.

Juliette hesitated. 'Go on,' said Muriel. 'You haven't forgotten Clifton and South Parade? Let me see, it was Maude Jeffreys who began it, wasn't it?'

'Who was Maude Jeffreys?' I asked.

'She was a beast,' said Juliette, and she stopped.

'Go on,' I said.

'I was only a child about eleven, and she was seventeen. I hated her and so did most of the girls. She was so strong, though, that they were afraid of her. All the bigger girls at school had little girl friends – minions they used to call them – who used to fag for them and . . . do other things.'

'Oh,' I said.

Juliette blushed. 'Well, Maude couldn't get anyone to be her minion till I came, and no one took me up – you were away that term, Muriel, with scarlet fever – and all the other girls had their minions, so she seized on me. I knew nothing at all then about things. I had come straight from home. Maude told me to fag for her, and as I saw the other girls of my own age fagging for the other big girls, I took it as a matter of course. They all seemed to like it, and got sweets and petted in return. Sometimes, too, the bigger girls called their minions to them after the lights were out and I used to hear kisses and soft words of endearment. I thought nothing of that, I only wished someone would pet me . . . but not Maude, I never wanted her to pet me, she was such a beast . . . she didn't wash, ugh!

'One day, after I had been at school a week, one of the bigger girls had cause to complain about her minion. Something or other had not been done to her liking, and when we went up to bed, I was surprised to be told not to undress at once. The other little girls evidently knew what was coming. The culprit was brought into my room – I slept in the biggest dormitory, with most of the little girls – and after a lecture from her senior, she was told to "go down". She was quite undressed and bent across a bed. Then her senior took a little cane out of her box and gave her about a dozen smart cuts on her little behind. The child sobbed and got up and went back to her own room. I was stupefied, but the rest of the girls seemed to like it and to take it as a matter of course. I was told I could now undress, and did so, feeling very nervous and uncomfortable. When I was in bed and the lights were out, I heard Maude calling me. I went over to her bed. "Get into bed with me," she said, "I want to talk to you." I did so very shyly. "You saw Elsie get whipped?" "Yes." "Well, that's what happens to naughty girls here, so be careful. If little girls don't do as they are told, their seniors whip them. How would you like me to whip you?" "Oh, Maude, please." "Well, mind you don't deserve it."

'I didn't like the turn the conversation was taking and moved to get out of bed, but Maude put her arm round me.

' "No, you are not to go yet. You've never been in bed with any of the other girls, have you?" "No." "Ah, well kiss me, kiddy." I didn't much want to, but I did as she said. I was surprised to find not only her lips but her tongue meet my lips. I drew back, but couldn't get away. Her hand moved down and began to pull up my nightdress. I could feel my cheeks burning with hot blushes. "You've got quite a nice little bottom for your age; it will be rather nice to smack." "Oh, Maude, don't . . . it's rude." She laughed. "Give me your hand." She took it, and before I knew what she was doing, placed it between her legs. "Don't take it away, but do as I do." She pulled my nightdress right up and roughly put her hand between my legs to . . . oh, how ashamed and frightened I was. "Oh, don't, please Maude, don't," I said, and tried to take her hand away. "Silly little fool, do as I tell you." But I was too upset and burst out crying. "Shut up, you idiot, or you'll be sorry. You shall pay for this tomorrow. Go back to your own bed." I crept miserably back and sobbed myself to sleep.

'The next evening Maude told me not to get into bed until she told me. She then called the other seniors together and explained the case, while I stood in my nightdress. She was not popular, but the rule at South Parade was strict. A senior had an unquestioned right to punish her minion, and though they didn't like her, the other seniors, for their own sakes, would not encourage insubordination in a minion. Besides, as I learnt afterwards, they all used their minions as Maude had tried to use me, and would not listen to any frightened protests on my part. So I had to bend over the bed, as I had seen the other little girl do the night before. Maude borrowed a cane and, lifting my nightdress, gave me ten hard cuts on my poor little behind. Oh, the pain and shame of that first whipping. I shall never forget it. I sobbed and twisted and kicked, but Maude held me down with one hand quite easily. All the time she was whipping me she was jeering at me. "Isn't it rude, eh, Miss Modesty? Fancy showing your nakedness to the whole dormitory."

'When she had finished she said: "Now go to bed and come to me when the lights are out." I crept into bed, and, soon after, the lights were out. I didn't move, but soon heard Maude calling me. As I didn't answer, she came across to my bed and roughly pulled down the clothes. She turned me over on my face and pulled up my nightdress and began whipping me again. I screamed but she kept my head pressed down into the pillow, which muffled the cries. She must have given me quite twenty or thirty before she stopped. "Now, will you come to my bed?" I was too hurt and frightened to resist any more and followed her miserably, and did all she told me to do.

'Oh, how I hated doing it, and hated her for making me. I was too young to get any pleasure myself and, as I said, she didn't wash.'

I laughed – I couldn't help it, and so did Muriel.

'It's all very well to laugh, but it was beastly.'

'I expect so,' I said. 'But go on.'

'Well, things went on like this. Maude was always getting into rows with the headmistress, Mrs Walter, and after getting punished herself used to get her own back on me. At last one day she was caught cheating in form and the whole school – there were about forty of us – were summoned to the big schoolroom. I knew Mrs Walter used to whip the girls, though up till then I had escaped, and the whippings were in private. This time, however, Mrs Walter came in to us and read us all a lecture on dishonesty and then called Maude out before all of us, and, after lecturing her, sent her away with the French mistress to get ready for punishment. She then told us to go into the punishment room. I had never been in this room, known as the Vale of Tears among the girls, before. It was a large empty room right at the top of the house. The only furniture it contained was a cupboard, a long narrow table with broad straps on either side, hanging down, a sort of vaulting horse, and a moveable scaling ladder fixed to one of the walls. There were forms round the side of the room, on which we girls sat and waited. After a minute or two, Mrs Walter came in with the other mistresses. She rang a bell and the door at the other end of the room opened and in came Mademoiselle leading Maude. The latter was a curious figure. She was naturally fat and lumpy, and her present costume did not improve her appearance. She wore a flannel dressing-gown, hind part in front, her face was blotched with fright, and she could barely walk. She looked such a ridiculous figure that in my astonishment and nervousness I giggled.

' "Who laughed," said Mrs Walter at once.

I stood up trembling.

' "Did you laugh?" "Yes, madam," I stammered, "I didn't mean to ... but Maude looks so funny." "Hm, she won't look funny soon. Let me see, you're a new girl." "Yes, madam." "Oh, and you have not been present at a punishment before? Well, let it be a lesson to you. Come here, Miss Jeffreys."

'Maude approached and stood trembling. "You were detected trying to copy your French exercises from the girl next to you." "Yes, madam." "Very good, you know what to expect?"

'She signed to the French and Second mistresses, who took hold of Maude and led her to the table and laid her face downwards on it, so that her legs hung over at one end, buckling the straps which hung on either side tight across her back, one just below her shoulders, one across her waist, and one just across her hips. Mrs Walter had gone to the cupboard and taken out a long cane. She came back to her victim and undid the dressing-gown. I realised now why it was backside front. As the buttons were undone, so it fell apart on either side, showing that Maude had on only a chemise. This was raised as high as possible and Maude's fat coarse behind fully exposed to view. Madam raised the cane to the full sweep of her arm and the first cut fell. I have never heard such a yell as came from Maude's lips. A second cut fell just in the same place, followed by another shriek. The older girls smiled. Maude was notoriously a coward. But Mrs Walter went on methodically with the whipping, taking no heed of the cries. Only when Maude began to kick, she said, "Keep still, or you shall be tied." But Maude's legs continued to fly about making a most indecent exposure. At last when she had given ten cuts, each of which had left its mark, Mrs Walter drew back and signed to the two mistresses and pointed to the horse. They wheeled that into the middle of the room, undid Maude, and led her to it. They bent her over it, and while one of them fastened her wrists to the two legs on one side, the other stretched her legs apart and tied her ankles to the other two legs. All that we girls could see was Maude's bottom wealed by the cane and her legs and what was usually hidden between. Mrs Walter now put back the cane and armed herself with a long birch. If the cane had made Maude yell with pain, the birch made her scream. But Mrs Walter took no notice. Down came the birch on the fat cheeks, until they were all crimson and purple. Quicker and quicker fell the blows, until at last most of the twigs had broken off and only a stump was left in her hands. Then she stopped and the mistresses undid Maude, who could scarcely stand, so shaken and weak with sobbing was she.

' "Will you cheat again?" "No, madam," she stammered, kneeling down. "Very good, take her away."

'That was the first whipping I saw at South Parade. We were dismissed and I noticed that most of the seniors retired to their studies with their minions. I was congratulating myself that I should be free from Maude for some time; the whipping would, I thought, keep her mind busy. But I was disappointed.

' "Maude wants you, Juliette, in the dormitory," said a small girl. I didn't dare not to go. I found Maude in bed sobbing. "Oh there you are, you little beast, are you? So you laughed at me, did you? Well, I'll pay you out for that, my girl, when I'm fit again. Now I want you to put some cream on my legs; you'll find some on my dressing table."

'I found some cold cream. Maude turned over on her face. "Pull the clothes down, and put it on, and mind you be gentle." I didn't relish the task of anointing her behind, you may be sure, but the sight of her battered flesh pleased me much. She lay and moaned the whole time, muttering abuse of Mrs Walter, until I had finished. That night she left me alone, she was too stiff and sore – though she had to show her behind to the whole dormitory (that was a custom of South Parade, and not even the biggest girls escaped doing it after a whipping). But the next night . . . I had to pay for laughing at her and she made me do everything to her, ugh.'

'Everything?'

'Yes, not only fingers . . . I had to . . . pah.'

'Poor little girl, but it didn't last, did it?' said Muriel.

'No, thank goodness, you came back and won me from her.'

'Won you?'

'Yes, that was a custom at South Parade. No senior could take a minion from another senior unless she won her. Sometimes seniors exchanged minions by agreement, but usually if a senior fancied a minion she had to fight for her and win her. Oh, it was quite a formal affair. The dormitory was cleared, a ring was formed, the minion was perched naked on a chest of drawers, and the two combatants, also naked, fought with knotted towels which they flicked at each other. No wrestling or holding was allowed. I shall never forget that fight for me. There was that fat ugly Maude with her coarse skin and dark thick hair, while you, darling, looked so frail beside her. Oh, I did hope you would win.'

'Well, what happened?'

'Oh, I won,' laughed Muriel. 'I'd had experience at home with my brother George. He'd learnt the game at school and used to practise on me in the holidays.'

'Oh, did he?'

'With our nightgowns on, of course, you naughty boy. Well, I'd learnt the trick of wetting the end of the towel and I could aim much better than Maude. I was quicker on my feet too, and she was such an awful coward. She nearly gave in after I had touched her once or twice on the thighs, and at last, when I got in a special cut of my brother's, right between her legs, she howled out: "Oh, take the little beast, I don't want her," and went to bed.'

'Yes, and you have had me ever since, haven't you?' said Juliette, flinging her arms round Muriel. 'I loved you then and I love you still, in spite of your cruelty to me sometimes.'

'But how? . . . Why? . . .'

'You mean, how does Juliette come to be here?'

'Ye–es, and . . .'

'And what?'

'Well, she was at school with you . . . but . . .'

'Oh, you mean you thought she was my maid. Oh, that's your mistake. She told me when you called that she was sure from your manner that you took her for the maid, and we agreed to keep it up as long as we could. No, she's my companion really. Tell him how it came about, Juliette.'

❧ 10 ❧

Juliette's Story – continued

'Well,' said Juliette, 'my father died suddenly and we were left awfully poor.'

'You must begin long before that,' said Muriel. 'It began with my leaving South Parade. You see, Maude never forgave me for winning Juliette from her and tried all she could to pay us out. There was no other little girl left without a senior, and no senior would share her minion with her, as was sometimes done. She didn't tell about the games at night in the dormitory, for that would have brought down on her head the vengeance of all the seniors, for we were all tarred with the same brush, and she was an awful coward. But she hated us both: Juliette because she could never get her to make love to her gladly, and me because she saw Juliette was quite eager to do anything to, or for, me. So things went on for about a year, until one hot summer's day in the garden I couldn't wait till night, and Juliette and I were having quite a nice little "flirtation" on the grass, which was rather long. Maude must have spotted us and told Mrs Walter, for we were suddenly startled in each other's arms by her voice: "What conduct is this?" There she stood looking down on us. "Get up at once, Juliette; do up your drawers, go and wash your hands and then come to my room." When we got there, she stormed at us, and talked about expelling us publicly. But I wasn't afraid of that.'

'Two hundred pounds a year each,' sniggered Juliette.

'Precisely. So she jawed a lot and at last said that in consideration for our parents, and the disgrace, etc., she would let us off with a flogging, but we must never do it again, would we promise? Oh, yes, of course, we would – and we never did – in the garden. She asked us if the other girls did the same sort of thing, and, of course, we said no, and then she asked me how I knew of such things. I said a servant at home. "I expected as much," she answered. Looking back now, I, of course, realise she was *one of us* herself, for she gloated over the details and her eyes glowed as she talked. Anyhow, we got our whipping – a private one, because she did not want to publish our disgrace and get the matter talked about, for fear of putting ideas into the girls' heads.'

'Was the whipping severe?'

'Pretty well, I'd had plenty in my time; she loved whipping me, she told me later, after I left school.

'She spanked you, didn't she?'

'Yes, she always spanked us little girls. She used to put us across her knees, turn our clothes up, let down our drawers, and use her hand or the back of a hairbrush. My word, it hurt, too, I couldn't sit down for over a week with any comfort.'

'But we paid Maude out, didn't we?'

'How was that?'

'Oh, that evening we held a court martial in the dormitory. We bribed the maid not to turn out the gas for half an hour, and we *tried* Miss Maude. Naturally all the seniors were eager to punish the sneak, and she was condemned to run the gauntlet and to be whipped by her two victims. It *was* fun. Picture this kid of twelve,' pointing to Juliette, 'laying into the fat behind of a girl of eighteen. "I can't hit hard enough," she nearly sobbed in her excitement, "I can't hurt her enough." I think, however, she managed pretty well, for Maude wriggled as we held her down. Then I had my turn; and at last she had to run naked three times up and down the dormitory between two lines of girls armed with canes. She was marked all over from her shoulders to her knees, both back and front, for she fell down more than once, and the blows never stopped. She didn't dare tell, however, and left at the end of the term, and so did I.'

'Before the next term began, Juliette's father died, as she told you, and when I heard of it, I got my mother to have her to stay with us, and be taught by my sister's governess. When mother died, and I was married, I still kept her with me as my sweetheart and companion – my old fool of a husband suspected nothing – and here we still are.'

'And she still lets you . . . '

'Whip her? Yes, habit is strong, and she never became a senior with a minion of her own.'

'I rather like that duel idea,' I said. 'I'd like to see one.'

'I dare say you would, but there's no minion to fight for \ . . . unless . . . ' and she looked at me.

'Unless what?'

'Unless you play the part of the minion; yes, that would do. You be the minion and Juliette and I will fight for you. Come on, Juliette, undress him and perch him up . . . We'll put him on the piano.'

They seized hold of me laughing and I let them strip me; then I stood on the baby grand piano, while they quickly took off their own clothes and got a couple of towels from the bedroom. The account of their school experiences had quite excited me, and I should have made quite a good scarecrow in a Roman garden.

There was certainly no *inutile liguum* about me, what there was was *utilissimus* in the highest degree.

They pushed the furniture back so that there was a clear space. 'Ready?' said Muriel. '*En garde.*' They held the towels in their right hands, crouching slightly forward. 'No hitting above the belt,' said Juliette. Muriel answered with a flick which just missed Juliette's right thigh. Quick as lightning Juliette flicked her towel upwards and just caught the brown curls.

'Little cat, that's the worst of teaching other people tricks.' She dodged and feinted and at last, seizing a favourable opportunity, made her towel curl round Juliette's left cheek with a resounding smack.

'Oo,' said Juliette and she clapped her hands to the place.

'First blood to me,' cried Muriel. Juliette said nothing but kept a wary eye on Muriel, lightly swinging the towel to and fro. Muriel feinted here and there and at last made a vicious cut at Juliette, but missed and overreached herself. That was what Juliette was waiting for. As Muriel stretched forward, she brought her towel twice in rapid succession straight up between her legs. Muriel leapt back out of reach and rubbed herself. Then, springing forward, she rained a perfect hail of blows on Juliette, caring nothing for the other's attacks. She parried with her left arm and flicked here, there and everywhere. Her quickness of wrist and eye surprised me. At last two cuts, one after the other, curled quite round between Juliette's cheeks, and as the latter retired, she followed them up with a couple of backhanders, both of which reached between Juliette's legs in front.

'Enough, enough, I give in,' cried Juliette, who was quite out of breath.

'Come on, Cecil, you're mine.' I jumped down. 'Get the cases, Juliette.'

'What,' I said. 'Do you think you're going to whip me?'

'Minions always are whipped . . . Do let me, just this once . . . you can whip me afterwards if you like . . . Besides, this is only a love whipping.'

'No,' I said. 'I tell you what. We'll have a triangular duel. I'll take the two of you on, and whoever gets the first cut home shall give his opponent five cuts. Towels or birches, you can choose your own weapons.'

'Towels for me,' said Muriel, 'they're longer.'

'Birch for me,' said I. 'Now, come on.' I waited for their attack and, as I expected, I easily dodged Juliette and parried Muriel's flick with my birch and, before she could recover, flicked her with the twigs between the legs.

'One; get down on the couch, Muriel.'

She obeyed. 'Not too hard, dear.' I gave her five moderate cuts and she got up.

'Round two,' I said. This time Muriel was not so eager; she kept a wary eye on my birch, so that I could not get her towel entangled in it. Juliette kept me busy flicking here and there. At last I thought I saw an opening and cut at her; I missed and quickly both towels came round me, one on either side. Muriel shouted for joy.

'Come on, Juliette, it's our turn now.' I could not in honour refuse or resist so, with as good a grace as I could, I lay down on the couch and took my five strokes from each of them. Neither of them tried really to hurt me, but made the birch curl wickedly between the cheeks and thighs.

'Round three, now look out Juliette.' She was evidently enjoying it and laughed. Cut and parry followed each other for a minute or two. I dodged this way and that and at last, more by accident, I fancy, than anything else, managed to flick Juliette's thigh. It was only just a graze, but it counted. She received her five strokes and wriggled with pleasure and pain.

We were all of us out of breath with laughing and the exertion. I threw myself into the chair. Muriel collapsed on the couch beside Juliette. The latter put her arms round her and hugged her. They certainly made a lovely picture with their bodies closely entwined. I sat and watched them, but the sight of their naked bottoms proved too much for me, and when I saw Juliette's right hand steal down between Muriel's legs, I got up softly and took the webbing from the case. Muriel's eyes were shut and Juliette lay half on top of her kissing her, her fingers very busy. I reached over them and before they knew what I was doing I had slipped the webbing underneath Muriel and tied them tight together. 'You naughty children,' I said in a gruff voice. 'I'll teach you. You're not at South Parade now,' and down came the birch on Juliette's plump little cheeks. She kicked and squirmed and, turning away to avoid the blows, brought Muriel's bottom into sight as she turned with her. I was not slow to take advantage of this new field of action.

'Mind my knuckles, though,' said Juliette as one cut reached between Muriel's legs.

'They shouldn't be there.' Muriel was now on top, and getting most of the blows. She had also got her hands round Juliette and was busily untying the knot.

She succeeded at last and, jumping up, ran to the case. 'Come on, Juliette, we'll pay him out for that trick.' They both seized birches and made for me. I had my work cut out to avoid them, and we all chased each other round the room slashing and cutting at each other with all our might. Very few of the blows proved effective, and at last, worn out with laughing and the chase, we all fell on the couch helpless. Then a less fierce but no less tiring orgy ensued, ending as usual in the bath. This, by the by, was built on the Roman plan of white marble with steps leading down into about four feet of water. It was a hobby of Muriel's husband, and was quite big enough for three or four people at the same time. It was more like the 'plunge' at a Turkish bath than the ordinary bath of today. The only drawback to it was that it took rather a long time to fill, and the water was never really hot. Still, as Muriel used to say, it was usually hot enough outside in her boudoir and it was good to have something to cool one.

❦ II ❧

Juliette's Story – concluded

'So, Juliette has been with you ever since she left school,' I said to Muriel after we had bathed and Juliette had gone to get tea.

'Yes, she came home to me, as I told you, to work with my young sister, and when I got married to Anthony, I had her with me as my companion and sweetheart, though Anthony never suspected that, and if he had, I shouldn't have cared.'

'But she's not a virgin and yet she never married, did she?'

'Ah! Now that's rather a tragedy, though it has its funny aspects. Would you like to hear about it?'

'Rather!'

'Well, we have long gaps in our family. I've one brother twelve years older than myself and one sister six years younger, and that's all. George was married when I left school and Elsie was quite a child, younger than Juliette. But I had a cousin Harry, just about Juliette's age, two years older, to be exact. He stayed with us one holiday when he was about seventeen. I was, of course, grown up and had "come out". Anthony was beginning to hang round, but he hadn't definitely proposed to me. Juliette and I were sweethearts, then as now, and though we did not share bedrooms, our rooms were next to each other, and you can imagine we spent most of the time in each other's arms. Harry evidently suspected our goings-on, as you will see, and he was as hot as you make 'em himself. But he was very clever. I never had the slightest suspicion, till the discovery. We used to be quite free and easy together. I used to tease him terribly, and delighted in seeing him grow uncomfortable and change his legs and move about on his seat. He told me afterwards that he didn't dare try any games on with me, although he wanted to badly. I was too grown up for him to tackle. But one night he saw Juliette going to my bedroom after we had all gone to bed, and he listened at the door. Our rooms were quite away from Mother's, and, as we never thought about Harry suspecting, we made no attempt to moderate our voices, and our exclamations of pleasure. He stood and listened at the door and heard everything, and I can assure you there was a good deal to hear. Luckily there was no whipping that night, or the sequel might have been different, but you can imagine he heard enough to leave no doubt as to what we were doing. Anyhow, the situation was too much for him, and, as he told me, he played a lone hand by himself on the mat outside and then, growing nervous lest he should be discovered, retreated to bed, where his sleep was not as undisturbed as it might have been.

'Looking back after the denouement, I remember that he looked most intently and meaningly at us the next day, but at the time I paid no attention to it. We played our usual game of hide-and-seek in the twilight in the garden, with the usual kisses for forfeits when caught. He certainly kissed me with more meaning than usual, but nothing more. With Juliette, however, he was much bolder, for she told me that his hand became very venturesome and once even tried, when he caught her, to investigate her most secret charms. Of course, at that time she was wearing shut-up drawers, so he couldn't get much satisfaction. She was very excited when she told me, and by no means as angry with him as I thought she ought to have been. I grew quite angry and jealous and threatened her with a whipping if she let it happen again. She promised she would not, but I determined to watch.

'That night I was prevented from my usual delights with Juliette by the ordinary periodical disability we poor women are cursed with, so Juliette knew it was no good coming to me. I was so angry and jealous, though, about her letting Harry take liberties with her, that I couldn't sleep, and I decided that I would give Juliette a whipping – not severe – but enough to relieve my feelings and to warn her as regards the future. So I got out of bed, took a birch from my trunk, where I always kept one safely locked up, and went to Juliette's room.

'When I got to the door I was thunderstruck at hearing voices. "Oh, don't, Harry, you're hurting me . . . no, don't . . . you can't get in, it's too big . . . use your fingers . . . no . . . no . . . no, I can't bear it . . . you're tearing me in two . . . oh . . . oh." I burst into the room and switched on the light. What a sight met my eyes. I could see nothing of Juliette, except her legs, which were wide apart, with the knees in the air, and between them Harry's back and bare legs, with the pyjamas round his ankles, moving vigorously up and down. Before he had time to stop I rushed to the end and brought the birch as heavily as I could down on his heaving buttocks. "You cad," I cried, "get off, how dare you violate that child?" He sprang off and away and I saw at a glance I was too late. Juliette's legs and mount were all red with blood, the damage had evidently been done. But I was just in time to prevent still worse mischief, for as he stood shamefacedly before me, great jets of his manhood spurted from his arrogant weapon. This was, of course, the first time I had seen a man in this condition, and I was naturally very excited. In fact I felt the bandage I was wearing was soaking with a different fluid from that for which I was wearing it. But I was too mad with anger and jealousy to pay much attention to that at the moment. I went to the door and shut and locked it and then turned to Harry, who was stooping to gather up his pyjamas. Juliette was still lying on her back, but she had turned her head away, covering her face with her hands and sobbing.

' "Now, what have you to say for yourself?" He remained mute. "I shall tell Mother of this the first thing in the morning, but that won't do much good. Juliette's ruined, you've taken her virginity, if you haven't seriously injured her. What reparation can you make? It's absurd to talk about marriage, you are both far too young. You beast, you cad," I raved at him, "how dare you corrupt an innocent girl?" "Not so much of the innocent," he broke in. "I'm sorry I took her maidenhead. I never thought she would have one." "What do you mean?" "Well, I listened at your door last night, and heard what was going on there between you and Juliette, so you see it's no good coming the innocent over me. And what's more, Miss Muriel, if you tell Auntie about me, I'll split on you two."

' "I don't know what you mean," I said, "but anyhow, she wouldn't believe you. We should both deny it, and that wouldn't do you any good. You would be sent home and if I know anything of Uncle Harry, you'll have the finest thrashing you've ever had in your life. Now I'll tell you what I'll do. I don't want any scandal. If you'll submit to be punished by me and promise faithfully not to do that to Juliette again – why, you might have given her a baby if I hadn't come in – and to marry her, if she will have you later, when you are in a position to marry – well, I'll say nothing to Mother. If you refuse, I go to Mother at once." "You punish me? How?" "With this, and a cane I've got. I mayn't be as strong as Uncle Harry, but I'll do my best." "I'm not afraid of you," he laughed, "you can do what you like to me, and as for

Juliette, I'll promise both those things." "Very good," I answered, "come here."

'I led him over to some hooks which were on the wall and made him catch hold of two of them. I found Juliette's stockings and tied each wrist as tightly as I could to a hook. His pyjama trousers were still round his ankles, and the short jacket, strained up by the position of his arms, left his bottom well exposed. "Now," I said, "we'll see whether I can do any good," and I rained a volley of blows with the birch all over both cheeks. He stood the punishment stoically, and I grew vicious. I became more deliberate, choosing my spot for the cuts carefully, and at last, one or two proved more efficacious, for he wriggled a bit and said, "Here, that'll do, Muriel."

'I laughed, "Do? I've not begun yet." I noticed that the birch was getting worn-out and, looking about me, saw Juliette's riding whip lying on the chest of drawers. It was a dainty little thing, quite light, but made of whalebone, bound with silk. I put down the birch and picked up the whip. The first cut right across both cheeks was evidently a surprise. He gave an involuntary cry of pain. "Here, what's that you're using?"

'He turned round to look as another cut fell just where the first had fallen. "Here, I say, that's enough." "Enough? Not half; I'll teach you to rape virgins. If I can't repair the injury, I'll make you suffer; your blood shall help to wipe out Juliette's. There, there, there and there. Don't you wish you had chosen Uncle Harry?" He made no attempt now to conceal his pain. "You'll cut me to pieces, you cat. Oh, oh, oh God," as a very vicious cut curled by chance between his plunging, kicking legs and flicked the hanging bag. His cries of pain spurred my energy. I redoubled my blows and his cries of pain and rage changed to sobs and appeals. 'Muriel, please no more; you'll cut me to bits; let me off now; I swear I'll marry Juliette. I'll never touch her again, Muriel, darling, for God's sake; oh, my God, have pity. Mercy, mercy, mercy."

'Juliette had somewhat recovered, and was sitting up watching the scene, frightened but excited. She had never seen such a whipping before. She joined her entreaties to his. "Oh, Muriel, don't hurt him too much. Look, his bottom's bleeding." She came to me and tried to stop me. I cut her across the bottom. "Don't you interfere, your turn will come next. I'll teach you to have a lover." She ran back to the bed, and I turned again to Harry. Certainly I had been severe. I must have given him over fifty cuts and his poor bottom and thighs were a mass of weals. Here and there the skin was cut, and there were little trickles of blood oozing down the skin. I felt just a little frightened, so I put aside the whip and took up the birch again. It had quite a different effect to what I expected. It must have hurt, but after the first few blows, Harry's cries changed in tone. Deep ahs and ohs followed each cut, but he no longer kicked and squirmed, he moved his loins backwards and forwards, just as I had seen him on the bed. I was interested and looked to see what he was doing. To my surprise, his weapon was rampant again and by his plunging he seemed to be trying to swing it up and down; his eyes were half-closed. In my curiosity I reached out my left hand to touch it. I just put my hand round it. "Oh, you darling," he murmured and plunged vigorously. Again the thick jets of life burst from him and he collapsed against the wall, hanging by his wrists.

'I was startled and not a little frightened, so I untied his wrists. He fell on me with his arms round my neck, sobbing and calling me his queen. He slid down on his knees and, bending down, kissed my feet, uttering all the time words of love and homage.

'This attitude completely conquered my anger. I raised him up. "That will do," I said, "we won't think any more about it. You can go to bed. Now, Juliette, for you."

' "You're not going to whip Juliette?" "Certainly I am." "No, you mustn't. It was all my fault. If you think she deserves punishment, punish me again for her. I'll bear hers as well as my own, if I can." He knelt down again and, flinging his arms round my legs, kissed my feet passionately.

'For the first time in my life I realised the ineffable joy of the woman dominant. I delighted in the subjection of Juliette, but she was only a girl and my minion. But here was a man, or at any rate a boy, absolutely subservient to me. I looked down on him as he grovelled before me, gloating over him, and exulting in my power. "Very well, then, Juliette shall escape for the present. You shall bear her punishment, and her humiliation. Take those pyjamas off." He did so. "Now kneel down before me there, and beg my pardon and ask me to whip you." He knelt down humbly. "Forgive me, Muriel," he sobbed. "Go on . . . ask for your punishment . . . ask for it." "Please whip me," he stammered. "Where?" I insisted. He looked up at me. "Wherever you like." "Oh, shall I flog your manhood?" His hand instinctively clasped his sex, protecting the tender parts. "Oh, no, not there." "Where then? On your bottom?" "Yes, on my bottom. See, there it is ready for you." And he bent forward pushing his bottom out, waiting for the strokes. "Kiss my feet, then, and keep still."

'I brought the remnants of the birch straight up and down between his cheeks six times, and at each blow he clasped my legs and kissed my feet ardently. His hands clutched convulsively round my calves, and when I stopped and raised him slightly, he did not let go but slid higher, pulling my nightdress up, until when he stood on his feet he had pulled it right up and held my naked body close to him. Our lips met in a long and passionate kiss. He was still sobbing from the pain; inarticulate words of adoration came from him and his touch was reverent though caressing.

' "Don't touch me there," I said suddenly, as his hand fell from my waist to where the bandage was fixed between my legs. "Why not, my queen of women? I worship every bit of you." "No, you mustn't, you ought not to have seen me like this." But it was no good, I could not stop him. His eager hand dived beneath the bandage and penetrated right into my most secret parts. He had not long to wait. The excitement of flogging him and his adoration had set my whole body on fire, and within a minute I drenched him with my life and love. I leant forward and kissed him frankly and lovingly.

' "You are forgiven, Harry, only remember your promises." "I will remember," he said, as he kissed me again. He then turned to Juliette. "Good-night, Juliette darling, forgive me for my unkindness to you, but you shall be my wife as soon as I can marry you." They kissed lovingly and he turned to go.

' "Don't forget those," I said, pointing to his pyjamas. "If they are found here in the morning, people will ask questions." He smiled, picked them up, and put them on.

'He winched a little as the flannel touched his wounded skin, smiled a little ruefully, kissed us both again, and went away to bed.

'That is how Juliette lost her virginity, Cecil.'

'But what about Harry? What became of him? He has not married Juliette.'

'No, he was drowned while bathing, poor boy, about a year after. How we've missed him. He was a natural masochist. I have never met anyone like him. My husband liked to be ruled, but that was because he was an old man and other pleasures had palled on him, but Harry loved my power over him. I hoped when I met you that you might have taken his place.' She gave a little sigh.

'But the boot is on the other leg,' I laughed.

'Yes,' she sighed, 'I never thought I could submit to the domination of any man, but you have conquered me, Cecil. I am yours utterly, my darling, my king.

'That's as it should be.'

'I don't know. It's all right for the present, but the future – I'm not a masochist, all my nature tends the other way, and I feel I shall want someone to subdue. Of course, there's Juliette, she's mine utterly, in spite of her revenge the other day. But I want a man – a man – '

'We must see if we can't find you one,' I laughed, 'provided always, of course, he doesn't interfere with my prerogative and privileges.'

'I shall always be yours, darling, no matter who there is.'

❧ ❦

Volume II

At the Seaside

London was growing very hot. For once in a way England had a summer worthy of the name. But for Muriel, I should have fled from the heat and lack of air of town long before. But the little house in South Molton Street offered far too great attractions to be deserted easily. However, one day when I called there, Muriel showed me a letter and asked me what I thought of it.

It ran as follows:

> DEAR MURIEL – The wife and I want to go globe-trotting for about six months or a year but we're in a difficulty about the two girls. Of course they're safe at school most of the year, but the question of their holidays bothers us. Would you be an angel and take charge of them, at any rate for the summer six weeks? You'll find them rather a handful, I'm afraid. The discipline at their school is not so good as it was for you at Clifton, and Gladys thinks they are too old to be corrected as you were, in the good old-fashioned way. But I dare say you will be able to manage them. Anyhow, if you will take them I give you *carte blanche* and will of course pay all bills. Do be a sweet sister and say they can come to you, and let us get out of England. They break up in a fortnight, so there's not much time.
>
> Always your loving brother,
>
> GEORGE

'What do you think of it?' said Muriel.

'Well, what were you going to do this summer?'

'I hardly know; of course, there are lots of people I could stay with, but the girls sound rather alluring, don't you think so? "Rather a handful" – *carte blanche* for me!'

'They'll be damnably in the way. If *they're* about I can't very well be on the premises. How old are they?'

'Young adults, I fancy. But of course you'll be on the premises. You can be a younger brother of my husband's if you like, or anything. The thing to do is to find a nice quiet little place where we can take a cottage or bungalow, quite by itself, where we can do just as we like. I bar all English watering places.'

'I know just the place you want, it's a tiny village called Croyde, in North Devon, just between Ilfracombe and Clovelly. I stayed at Woolacombe one summer – that's just round Baggy Point – and drove over to Croyde. It's perfectly beautiful. And there are two cottages right on the beach with no other house for quite two hundred yards.'

'It certainly sounds lovely; but how can we get to know about the cottages, whether they are to let, and how soon?'

'I'll run down and prospect.'

'Do, there's a good boy, and I will write and tell George I'll take the girls off his hands.'

I went down to Woolacombe next day and found a house agent at Morthoe. By the greatest of good luck, the cottages had fallen vacant suddenly, and I was able to take them for two months. So a week later saw Muriel, Juliette and me surrounded with luggage – the *cases* naturally were not forgotten – on Morthoe station waiting for the 'jingle' and cart to take us and our belongings to Croyde.

We had decided to dispense with servants; the wife of the coastguard was to come in and cook breakfast and dinner, but the rest of the day we were to do for ourselves so as to have perfect freedom.

Muriel had written a 'leading' letter to her brother about the management of her nieces, and his reply was quite explicit:

I give you absolute authority to manage both Gladys and Ethel as you think best. In your own case, I know the strict discipline of Mrs Walter was most advantageous. My wife had no such Spartan training and consequently suffers. But both the girls take after our family, I fancy, and will be all the better for a firm hand.

Muriel's eyes glistened as we read this letter together, and we looked forward to the girls' coming eagerly.

They arrived, the first week in August, having seen their parents off to Hamburg on their way round the world.

Gladys was plump and fair, just budding into womanhood. Her breasts were beginning to swell and the rounded hips gave promise of a most voluptuous figure when fully developed. Ethel was a slight dark girl, straight and lissom, a regular tomboy, and young for her age.

They were both very excited at the prospect of a holiday away from father and mother and kissed their aunt and Juliette most affectionately. Me they greeted quite frankly, though Gladys gave me what was suspiciously like 'the glad eye'.

'Now girls,' said Muriel, 'we're going to have a splendid time, this is the land of do-as-you-like, no lessons, no one else to consider, only enjoyment and fun – bathing, lazing, exploring, sailing all day long. Only one thing, we must be punctual at meals, and when bathing we must be careful not to go out too far.'

'Can we bathe now, Auntie?' said Ethel eagerly.

'Not tonight,' said Muriel, 'it's too late, but tomorrow morning early we'll all bathe before breakfast.'

Ethel looked glum. 'Oh, I want to bathe now.'

'No, wait till tomorrow, dear.'

Gladys gave her sister a glance. 'Mother would let me bathe now,' insisted Ethel. 'I *want* to bathe now.'

'Ethel dear, you must do as you are told; don't make me angry with you the first evening. Come, let's play Coon-Can.'

'I want to bathe now.'

'Shut up, Ethel, don't be silly,' said Gladys. But Ethel still looked sulky.

'Ethel,' said Muriel, 'we'd better understand each other straight away; you must do as I tell you, or we shall quarrel. Your father has put me in charge of you and given me complete control of you. Now we can be quite happy all of us together if you are obedient – you won't find me strict in all reasonable things – but you must obey me, otherwise I'm afraid you will have to be treated like a naughty girl and punished, and we don't want punishments on a holiday.'

Though her tone was as soft as honey, there was a gleam of expectancy in her eyes as she glanced at me that boded ill for Miss Ethel in the future.

The latter said no more at the time, and we played cards until we went to bed.

Next morning, I woke early and, putting on my bathing suit, called out to the others. Before long they appeared in mackintoshes and ran down the beach to me in the surf. Muriel and Juliette's figures I knew well. Gladys looked a perfect picture. Her dress revealed every graceful line of her slim young body, and though, as I realised by the quick glance she gave my person, she evidently was not altogether ignorant of the difference of sex, there was still a fresh innocence about her carriage that was more than disquieting to me, clad as I was in a tight varsity costume. Ethel on the other hand simply revelled in her freedom from petticoats. There was no very marked fullness of the breasts as yet, but her legs were beautifully shaped and her plump little bottom filled her bathing suit admirably.

'Oh, Auntie!' she said. 'I do wish I could wear my bathing suit all day, it's so much nicer than those horrid petticoats.'

Muriel laughed.

'For shame,' said Gladys, looking self-consciously at me.

'Do let me, Auntie.'

'Well, perhaps, during the morning on the beach, if no one else is about.'

We romped and swam about in the surf – there is not much chance of real swimming on the North Devon coast – until at last, just as we were about to get out, a big wave caught Gladys unexpectedly, and bowled her right over. Her legs went right up in the air wide apart. The stockinette was semi-transparent now it was soaked through, and I caught a glimpse of all her secret charms, half-concealed, half-revealed by the clinging material. More than that, her struggles underwater, to regain her feet against the undertow, burst the top button of the costume and she appeared with it open nearly to her waist. 'Oh, look at Gladys, showing her titties,' shouted Ethel in high glee. Gladys covered in confusion, with a quick glance at me, ran to the mackintoshes, slipped one on, and flew to the cottage. But she was not quick enough to escape my keen and watchful eye. The bathing dress gaped wide open and, as her sister said, showed both her budding little breasts, firm and plump and round.

In spite of the chill of the water, the blood raced through my veins and I felt my costume growing tighter and tighter as John Thomas asserted his presence in a quite unmistakable manner. Muriel turned to Ethel, 'What did you say?'

'Gladys was showing all her titties!' she laughed.

'How dare you say such a thing, you rude girl!' And before Ethel knew what was happening, Muriel had seized her under one arm and, turning her behind up, gave her several sounding slaps on the tight little bottom.

'Don't you dare say such a thing again.' Ethel was more surprised than hurt, but she was evidently very angry at the ignominious treatment. She wriggled away and darted a vindictive glance at Muriel and ran up the beach shouting out, 'Gladys showed her titties.'

I looked at Muriel. 'This must be settled,' she said to me. 'Juliette, bring Ethel to me when she is dressed. *You* had better keep out of the way for a bit as it's the first time.'

I didn't like this, you may be sure, but thought it wiser to comply, so, went to my room, shaved and dressed leisurely. As I was brushing my hair I heard Muriel's voice lecturing Ethel. I could not quite catch the words, but I heard Ethel say, 'What! Whip me! I've never been whipped in my life! You shan't, I tell you. You shan't.' There were the sounds of a struggle and then, 'You shan't take my drawers down. Gladys, help, help – oh!' This last exclamation was preceded by the sound of a smack. From the sound, I guessed Muriel was using the back of a hairbrush. The smacks went on, so did the cries – angry at first, but soon a note of pain crept in and at last real sobs took their place. Oh, how I longed to be there! I pictured to myself the round little bottom growing pinker and pinker under the blows. I saw in my imagination the little cheeks contract and loosen as the brush fell upon them – the ineffectual struggles – the plunging and heaving of the young body. The cries and sobs kept time with the crisp smacks which fell quicker and even quicker as Muriel warmed to her work. I heard Muriel's voice raised above Ethel's sobs. 'I'll teach you to talk before gentlemen about your sister's titties! How dare you, you saucy little minx! Will you ever be rude again? Will you? Will you? Will you?'

By this time Gladys had evidently come down, for I heard her voice, 'Oh, Auntie!'

'Ethel was very rude just now about you, before Mr Prendergast, and I had to punish her.'

'Yes, I know, I heard her; but isn't she rather big for a whipping? Mother never has whipped us.'

'So I learn from your father. So much the worse. But don't you make any mistake, I was whipped till I was eighteen or nineteen at school. So you see, even you are not too old if you deserve it.'

I did not hear any reply from Gladys and thought it was time I showed myself. I ran downstairs and came into the room as if nothing was happening. Muriel was sitting quite calmly. She had evidently had Ethel across her knee, for her dress had been pulled slightly up and showed one leg nearly to the knee. Gladys was standing just inside the door, looking rather frightened, while Ethel was turned away with her hands over her face, sobbing with anger and pain.

'Hullo! What's up?' I asked quite innocently, as if I knew nothing and had heard nothing.

'Ethel was naughty and I had to punish her.'

'Oho,' I said.

'Yes, she has been properly punished, but I think it's done her good.

Come here, Ethel, and kiss me and say you're sorry.'

Ethel didn't move. 'Shall I have to give you some more before Mr Prendergast?'

'Oh no, no.'

'Then come here at once, kiss me and say you are sorry . . . That's better. Now do your drawers up and we'll have breakfast.'

During the meal, Ethel did not dare look at me, but Gladys ever and again cast half-frightened glances at me and at her aunt and at Ethel. It was altogether rather an awkward meal. When it was over, Muriel called Gladys to her and said, 'Perhaps you had better see your father's letters to me about you two,' and she took them from her writing-case. 'There, you see he says you are a handful and that I have *carte blanche* as regards keeping you in order. Now I've told you that I was whipped when I was even older than you, so you know what you may expect if you are naughty.' She gave her a playful smack on her bottom which sent the red flag flying in Gladys's cheeks, kissed her lightly on the lips and let her go.

We bathed again during the morning. It was gloriously hot and we lolled about on the sand still in our bathing costumes. Muriel was careful to show Ethel that with the punishment the fault was wiped out and forgotten. She was perfectly sweet to her and by degrees won her round from her shyness and self-consciousness. After a while she and Juliette and Ethel went scrambling over the low rocks and pools looking for crabs and fishes as the tide went out. Gladys and I were left together lying on the sand.

I saw her looking at me now and then, furtively, and waited. At last she said, 'Uncle Cecil.' We had arranged that she should call me that.

'Well?' I said.

'Uncle Cecil, I want to ask you something.'

'Well?'

'Do you think Auntie meant what she said about being whipped when she was older than me?'

'I'm sure she did.'

'I can't believe it. I'm sure I should die of shame, if I was whipped. When I came in this morning, when Auntie was whipping Ethel, I felt as if I should sink through the floor.'

'Why?'

'Oh, Uncle, she was lying across Auntie's knee and she was all uncovered. All her things were undone.'

I smiled.

'Oh, Uncle, she wouldn't do that to me, surely?'

'I don't suppose she would put you across her knee, you're too big; but I'm quite sure that if you are naughty you'll have to suffer for it – there.' I patted the cheek of her bottom, which I could just reach as she was lying half-turned on her face. She blushed fiery red and rolled over, away from me, showing the lines of her breasts and hips. Her costume, still wet, clung to her and revealed all her form. The pink of her skin showed through, and I could trace the pit of her navel and the swelling of her mount. She noticed my eye roaming all over her and drew her mackintosh round her. I was on fire. I turned towards her. 'Why should you be so afraid and shy of being whipped?' My arm went round her and I drew her towards me; she let herself go and looked shyly yet provokingly at me. 'I'm sure you've nothing to be ashamed of, there's plenty to smack here,' as my hand caressed her bottom.

'Oh don't, Uncle!' My hand moved away and stroked her thigh and at last met the end of her torso and the valley between the thighs. A little sigh escaped her lips, and she edged a little closer to me. 'Oh, Uncle,' she whispered, and she let her head fall on my shoulder.

I gave a quick look round to see that Muriel and the others were out of sight and, finding we were quite alone, pushed my hand between her legs and began to tickle the soft lips which I could feel through her costume. She made no resistance, she even opened her thighs slightly as if she knew what was to come and wanted it. Her face turned up to mine, her lips half-opened and, just as I felt her whole nature give and yield to my caresses, our lips met in a burning kiss. 'Gladys,' I said half-sternly, 'that wasn't the first time! You've been playing naughty games at school; now tell the truth, haven't you?' I made her look at me.

'Yes,' she whispered, 'but that was only with girls; it's the first time with a man. Oh, it was lovely.'

'Well, you had better not let Muriel know of these goings on, or your bottom *will* have to pay for it.'

'Hm, I suppose she's greedy and wants it all for herself; *I* know.' I thought it better to say nothing, especially as I saw the other three coming towards us over the rocks.

'We've got such a funny fish,' shouted Ethel, running towards us. We sat up and waited. Muriel looked keenly at both of us, and as soon as I could I got her away by herself. 'What have you been doing?' she asked.

'Breaking the ice for you,' I answered.

'Mind you don't go breaking anything else,' she said. 'I won't have *that*. If she's a virgin now, she shall leave me the same.'

'That's all right,' I said, 'we only talked about whipping, she's very frightened, but I think it will be possible.

Muriel's eyes gleamed.

'It would be lovely to whip her, wouldn't it?'

'Yes, but I must be there, no more tantalising experiences like this morning.'

'Poor boy, was he unsatisfied then? It's a shame,' and she laughingly seized hold of a certain part of me and squeezed it hard.

'You little devil, I'll pay you for that tonight when the girls are in bed.'

⁍ 2 ⁌

Fun on the Beach

After dinner, which we had in the middle of the day so that Mrs Tasker, the coastguard's wife, could get away home, it was very hot. I was in flannels, Muriel and Juliette in light linen dresses with nothing much underneath from all appearances, Gladys wore the usual schoolgirl serge skirt and blouse and Ethel a little holland frock with a loose belt. 'What are we going to do this afternoon, Auntie?' she asked.

'I'm going to rest, it's too hot for exertion, but you two can do what you like.'

'May we paddle?'

'Certainly. You'd better go with them, Cecil, and keep them out of mischief, and mind, on no account be late for tea.' She gave me a meaning look as she said this.

'May I take these things off and wear my bathing dress?' said Ethel. 'These are so hot.'

'No, dear, not today. There may be some strangers about.'

'We haven't seen any all the morning. Well, I needn't wear my petticoat, need I?'

Taking silence for consent, she ran upstairs and came down again after a minute or two. 'That's better, come along Gladys and Uncle

Cecil.' So we started; the tide was right out and we ran over the wet sand, Ethel careering here, there and everywhere, her skirt as she ran showing every line of her slim young legs. None of us was wearing socks or stockings and her white legs gleamed in the sun. Gladys and I followed more sedately. 'Hurry up, lazybones,' shouted Ethel when she reached the sea, 'it's lovely.' I rolled my trousers up to my knees, and Gladys raised her skirts demurely, holding them tightly round her legs. Ethel, however, took no precautions as regards modesty. She danced and skipped about, jumping up as the waves came in. Naturally her skirt flew up at moments showing the white thighs, but there were no signs of any knickers. At last, in dodging a bigger wave than usual, she lifted her skirt quite high and I realised she had nothing on underneath it. Gladys evidently noticed it too, for she called out, 'Ethel, come here, I want you.'

'What is it?'

'I want to say something to you.' Ethel came to her sister, who whispered something to her.

'Yes, I've taken 'em off,' shouted Ethel in high glee. I saw Gladys blush crimson.

'How can you be so rude, I shall tell Auntie.'

'Tell-tale cat.' Here she ran off again.

'What's the matter?' I asked, though guessed the truth.

'Ethel's taken off all her things. She's got nothing on under her skirt.' She blushed furiously as she spoke; it might have been her own nakedness that was in danger of exposure.

'Well, there's no one to see that matters. And you don't seem to have much on yourself.' I ran my hand over her rounded hips and legs.

'I'm properly covered, at any rate.'

'Even though everything can be seen,' I interjected.

'You *are* naughty, Uncle Cecil.'

We had passed beyond the low ridge of rocks and had reached a little cove, out of sight of the cottage, with no outlet inland. At high tide the sea came right up to the cliff, but now with the tide out a lovely smooth stretch of sand was growing dry and hot in the sun. I flung myself upon it and took out a pipe. Gladys sat down beside me, clasping her knees with both hands. Ethel was still dancing around. I closed my eyes in perfect content, thinking how I could lead Gladys on to the subject which Muriel and I had at heart, and yet not shock her too much. *Festina lente* ran through my mind, but for the life of me I didn't know how to begin.

My reverie was startled by the sound of a struggle quite near. 'Don't

Ethel, you little wretch,' said Gladys. I opened my eyes just in time to see Ethel seize Gladys's shoulders from behind and pull her back. Naturally she rolled right on to her back with her legs in the air. She only had on a pair of thin cotton bloomers. She grabbed hold of Ethel's leg and brought her down on top of her. For a minute there was a whirl of legs and bodies. Ethel's frock flew right up, showing all her legs and body right up to her waist. Shrieks of delight came from her, as Gladys wrestled with her and tickled her. There was no attempt or pretence to hide her nakedness. She kicked and flung her legs apart as she strove to escape from her sister's grasp. At last she managed to get on top for a moment, showing to my enraptured gaze the plump little cheeks. I couldn't resist the temptation, and brought my open hand down on them with a loud smack. 'Who did that?' she shouted, and wrenched herself away from Gladys and flung herself on to me. In a minute we were all three in a kicking, tangled *mêlée*. My hands were very busy wandering everywhere. Gladys and Ethel shrieked with laughter as I tickled them under the arms, in the ribs, just by the hip bones and – whenever I got a chance – between their legs. I was careful, however, not to make it too obvious that I was aiming there particularly. They retaliated on me, joining forces against the common enemy. We rolled about, struggling and laughing. Suddenly I felt the top button of my trousers go. I was, of course, wearing no braces, and knew what would happen in a short time. My shirt worked up and at last Ethel discovered a small triangle of bare skin at the side by the waist. She redoubled her efforts at this particular point. The gap became bigger and she shrieked with glee as her hand explored round my waist under the loose canvas shirt. I made no attempt to stop her but groped all over her under her skirt, and openly tickled Gladys's legs and stomach with my other hand as she lay half under me. They both were carried away by the excitement. At last when my fingers reached and fastened on Ethel's narrow little slit she giggled and squirmed. 'You rude thing, if you tickle me there, I'll tickle *you* there.' Her little hand dived easily down and found what was evidently a surprise to her. She gave a gasp of astonishment as she felt her fingers clasping my rampant engine. 'Oh, whatever's that?' I ripped open my fly and out sprang his Lordship in magnificent state. 'Oh, what a funny thing. Gladys, look!'

Gladys, who was going off into an ecstasy under my skilful fingers, raised herself and, seeing what was exposed, buried her face on my shoulder. 'Look, Gladys, look; isn't it funny?' as she played with it. This was too much for John's self-control. He swelled and throbbed and sputtered. 'Oh, the nasty thing,' said Ethel, drawing her wet hand away. 'What's it doing?'

'You little devil,' I said in mock anger, 'I'll teach you,' and I laid her across my knee, turned up her skirt and spanked her, not hard but caressingly. She laughed and shouted and wriggled, and tried to pull down her skirt. Gladys sat up and tried to get her away from me. I let her go but kept hold of Gladys herself, and in a minute she was occupying her sister's position; my nimble fingers undid the bloomers and pulled them down, and quick smacks fell on the soft rounded cheeks. 'Oh, Uncle!' she exclaimed in a shy shocked tone, but she made no real effort to get away. She lay right across my knees, or rather lap, and felt my still-aggressive old man pressing against her smooth little belly. She wriggled and squirmed and at last I felt my hand bedewed with the warm creamy flow of her passion.

Ethel stood looking on laughing. 'Who's a rude girl now?' she jeered. 'What's the good of wearing drawers if they get taken down? Nobody can take mine down, I've got none to take.' In her excited precocity she held up her skirt round her waist and danced about showing all her nakedness.

Gladys got up. 'Ethel, for shame!' Ethel rushed to her sister. The force of her attack brought Gladys down again and I saw Ethel's hand go straight up her sister's clothes and begin to probe and feel her most secret parts. 'Oh, you've come already!' she said to my surprise, for I didn't suppose she knew as much. 'I haven't. Do it to me.'

'Ethel, be quiet, with Uncle Cecil here.'

'No I won't.'

'Uncle Cecil make her stop. Smack her, make her get up.'

I didn't disobey, and my smacks grew harder.

'That's enough, that hurts,' said Ethel. 'I don't want two whippings in one day, my bottom's still sore from Auntie.' She got up rubbing her little bottom with both hands. 'It *does* smart.'

'It'll smart still more if your auntie finds out you've come out dressed like that.'

'Oh, I'll run upstairs when I get home and put my knickers on, before she finds out. Ooh,' she giggled, 'I wonder what she'd say if she knew what we'd been doing this afternoon.'

'She'd make us all smart, I expect,' I said.

'Not you, she couldn't whip you, you wouldn't let her.'

'Well, I should probably have to go away, and she'd whip both of you.'

'Then she mustn't know, must she Gladys! Uncle Cecil mustn't go away.'

'No,' said Gladys. And they both flung their arms round my neck and kissed me. I pressed them both in my arms.

'Come on, girls,' I said to them, 'it's getting late. We must get home to tea!' I did my trousers up and Gladys fastened her bloomers.

'Wait a minute,' said Ethel. 'I want to go somewhere.' She ran behind a low rock and squatted down. We could hear the hissing of the stream against the rock and saw it trickle round, down the sloping sand.

'Oh, isn't she rude?' said Gladys, blushing.

'Come along.' We hurried down the beach and Ethel ran after us and caught us up. The tide had turned and was running; when we got to the barrier of rocks which separated this cove from Croyde, we had to wade. My height enabled me to get through fairly well. I could stretch from rock to rock, but Gladys and Ethel found it much more difficult. They both lifted their skirts around their waists, but Gladys's bloomers got very wet, and once Ethel slipped and, in trying to save herself, let her skirt go and consequently was soaked to the skin. 'That's done it,' she said as she scrambled out. 'Just my luck.' Her wet skirt clung to her legs, showing clearly that she had nothing on underneath. Gladys noticed it too.

'You'd better go up and change quickly,' she said, 'before Auntie sees you. She can't help seeing you've only got a skirt on.'

We hurried on, hoping to escape Muriel's keen eyes. But she was waiting at the door, watch in hand. 'Ten minute late,' she said as we came up. 'This won't do. I won't have meals kept waiting . . . Why, whatever have you been doing? . . . Come here' – to Ethel – 'you're wringing wet, go and change at once.' Ethel started to go quickly; the wet skirt clung to her. Muriel stopped her. 'Stop a moment,' she put her hand on her hip and then under her skirt. 'Why, where are your clothes?'

'I didn't wear any, Auntie, it was so hot.'

'What!' said Muriel, working herself up into a rage. 'You disgusting, rude little girl. Do you mean to tell me you dared to go out with your uncle with nothing on under your skirt? Gladys, how dared you let her?'

'I didn't know, Auntie, until we got down to the sea.'

'Well, why didn't you send her back? I'd have given her a good whipping, and made her dress properly. Now – you're just as bad as she is. I'm surprised at you, a great girl of your age. Go upstairs both of you and change. I'm very angry with you. I hope, by the by, *you* are more decently dressed than your sister.'

'Oh yes, Auntie.'

'Come here, and let me see.' She caught hold of her and pulled her skirt up in spite of Gladys's protests. 'Hm, that's something in your favour, but it won't altogether save your bottom.' Gladys started but did not say anything, and the two girls went indoors.

Muriel turned to me with eager eyes. 'Well!' she said. 'Everything is going on splendidly.' I whispered and told her all that had happened. She gloated over the story. 'Oh, won't I whip them!'

'You can't do *that*,' I said. 'You are not supposed to know. If they suspect for a moment that I told you, I should lose their confidence. They must never guess, at any rate not yet a while, that we are in league together. No, what must happen is something like this. You whip them tonight for Ethel's going without drawers. I can't be there, damn it, but I will listen outside the door, then when you've all gone to bed I will go into them and condole with them. You can come in and find us and . . .'

'And I whip you all three!' said Muriel eagerly.

'Yes, I suppose I shall have to go through it,' I smiled. 'But it will be worth it for once. I owe you a whipping already, you know, so we shall be quits before the night's out . . . Look here, when you find us you must order me to go away at first, leave the place, etc., and then relent and offer me the choice of a whipping, see?'

'Right you are,' she answered, 'and God help your bottom if you choose it; I must make the most of my chances these days. Come on into tea and we'll tell Juliette.'

'You had better not be too severe with them the first whipping,' I said. 'Wait for the second whipping for that. Go slow.'

'You leave it to me,' she smiled back. 'I won't tire myself out; I shall have your bottom to look forward to, and shall want some strength left for that. Oh, what a glorious night it will be!'

❦ 3 ❦

The Sequel

Tea was rather a quiet meal. There was an air of nervous constraint over all of us. Ethel wore a look of rather nervous defiance, darting ever and anon mutinous glances at Muriel. Gladys was evidently very anxious, and timidly looked, now at me, now at Muriel, as if trying to read what was in store for her, in her aunt's eyes. The latter preserved a distant demeanour which amused me considerably. I knew she was eager to get to work, and whenever she met my eye, I saw a gleam in hers which was instantly repressed when she found Gladys looking at her. The silence became oppressive and evidently got on Gladys's nerves. She seemed to have lost all appetite, her food seemed to choke her. Her face alternately flushed and paled. Muriel noticed her nervousness and pressed food on her. But she shook her head and managed to answer, 'No thank you, Auntie.'

'Come, don't be silly, Gladys; even if you have been naughty, I don't want you to starve as a punishment; my methods are quite different from that,' she added maliciously. This hint was too much for the girl; she buried her face in her hands and sobbed aloud. 'What's the matter, you silly baby,' said Muriel, getting up and putting her arm around her.

'Oh, Auntie, I'm frightened.'

'There's nothing to be frightened about.'

'But you're going to – to – '

'What?'

'To whip me,' she stammered.

'Of course I am; you've been very naughty, and I shouldn't be doing my duty if I didn't correct you. But you're surely not frightened at the idea of a whipping, are you? A big girl like you.'

'It's the shame of it, I've never been whipped and it sounds so awful.'

'Nonsense, don't be silly. You'll make me really very angry if you talk like that. Perhaps we'd better not wait till bedtime, as I had intended, but get it over at once. Then you can go to bed and by today morning we shall all have forgotten all about it. Cecil, if you've finished your tea, perhaps you wouldn't mind going out for half an hour.'

I got up at once, and said good-night to the two girls.

Ethel still looked mutinous but said nothing; Gladys clung to me for a moment. I whispered, 'Courage, it will soon be over,' and went out of the cottage but, as may be imagined, did not go far away.

I gave Muriel about three minutes for her preparations and then crept back to the open window. The blind was down so I could listen quite safely without being seen. It was exasperating not to be able to see, but that pleasure I promised myself before long. Juliette had evidently fetched the cases down, for Muriel was beginning to lecture Ethel. 'Now Ethel, come here and stand before me. You know what I am going to whip you for. For disgraceful indecency. You dared to go out with your sister and uncle with practically nothing on. From the state of your clothes when you came back, you must have been in the water up to your waist; so you must have exposed all your nakedness, for your skirt must have been lifted up by the waves. Wasn't that so?' Ethel evidently wouldn't answer. 'Wasn't it so, Gladys?'

'Yes, Auntie.'

'Ah well, you evidently don't mind showing those parts which modesty should make you careful to conceal, so you can pretend to no shame now. Take your drawers off and come here . . . Will you do as I tell you? Take them off at once.'

'I won't.'

'Oh won't you? Well, so much the worse for you. Juliette, take them off and bring her to me.'

There were the sounds of a scuffle and I heard Ethel's voice, 'Gladys, don't let them, save me.'

'If you do, Gladys, it will be the worse for you when your turn comes.' Gladys evidently thought discretion the better part of valour, for I heard Ethel cry out almost at once, 'You shan't, I won't be whipped, I won't, I won't.'

'Take them right off,' said Muriel. 'Now hold her legs . . . Now, Ethel, you see it's no use resisting; the more you struggle the worse will be the whipping. I'm sorry to have to do this the first day you are here, but you must be taught not to show this naughty little bottom to gentlemen. It is only meant to be seen when it deserves to be whipped – whipped – whipped.' From the sound of the smacks, Muriel was evidently spanking her with her hand. Ethel made no sound. The smacks became quicker and evidently hurt Muriel as well as Ethel, for I heard her say, 'Juliette, give me that little cane.' The first cut brought a little shriek from Ethel. 'Ah, I thought that would prove more effective.

Now, you naughty little girl, will you – will you – will you show your nakedness to your uncle again? Will you? Will you? Answer me when I ask you.'

'Oh, Auntie, don't, don't. I can't bear it, don't, don't.'

'Take your hand away and answer me. Will you be good and modest in the future? Will you? Will you?'

'Oh yes, yes, please stop. I *will* be good, oh don't whip me any more, don't, don't.'

'This naughty bottom must be taught the danger of being seen. There, there, there.'

'Oh, Auntie, I *will* be good, oh let me go, Auntie, please. I *will* be good. Oh! oh! oh!' These last three cries followed three particularly cutting strokes, which evidently were the crowning mercy.

'There, that will do, I think, for this time, and I hope it will do you good. Now stand up and put your drawers on and go to bed. Say good-night to Juliette and me. Kiss me; there now, we won't think any more about it.' I heard Ethel's sobs and the sound of a kiss. 'You'll be a good girl, now?'

'Yes, Auntie.'

'That's right. Good-night, dear.' I heard the door close and the steps go upstairs; a light appeared in the bedroom window.

I heard Muriel's voice again. 'Now, Gladys, for you. You've seen me whip Ethel for being naughty, and though you were not quite so much at fault as she was, still you were naughty. Why didn't you send Ethel back to dress properly? You are quite old enough to know better. I should have been ashamed myself to have let my sister show herself like that to a gentleman. What have you to say for yourself?'

'I'm sorry, Auntie, I didn't think.'

'No, quite so; well, you must be taught to think . . . Ah, that will do. Bend over the end of that couch. Turn your skirt up first.'

'Oh, Auntie, I don't like to.'

'I dare say you don't, but you must . . . Higher than that . . . oh, I didn't know you wore those . . . undo them.'

'Oh, Auntie, I can't, it's so shameful, let me keep my bloomers on, whip me over them.'

'Don't be silly, Gladys. Juliette, undo those knickers.'

'Oh, Auntie, please, please . . . '

She evidently had cast herself at Muriel's feet, for I heard the latter say, 'Get up at once, don't kneel like that, but do as I tell you or you'll make me more angry. Juliette, lift her up and bend her over the couch.' Whack! I heard the first cut of the cane fall across the firm flesh. If Ethel's whipping had excited me, my feelings at this point may be imagined. My imagination was on fire, I cursed my luck at not being able to be present; in my mind I saw the dainty bottom and thighs laid bare with the flap of the knickers hanging down. I could barely restrain my feelings; suddenly it occurred to me that the couch was against the wall immediately opposite the window; if I lifted the blind or pulled it aside, I ought to be able to see something. No sooner thought than done. The cuts followed each other methodically. Muriel was not, as usual, interpolating remarks to her victim, whose sobs and cries for mercy were the only other sound to be heard. I carefully pulled the edge of the blind away from the window and, to my joy, found that the scene was being played right before me. There was poor Gladys, held down by Juliette, her lovely moons facing me. The cuts had not been too hard, for scarcely any marks showed. Here and there a dull pink line appeared, but Muriel had evidently remembered our conversation. But now the whipping was evidently coming to an end; quicker and quicker came the cuts, more and more imploring the cries. 'Oh, Auntie, spare me, spare me, mercy, mercy; oh, I can't bear any more, oh, Auntie, don't.'

'Don't kick like that, or you will get more. These are the last five – one – two – three – four – five . . . let her get up, Juliette.' Juliette took her hand away from Gladys's back, but the latter still lay there sobbing, and twisting her poor wounded cheeks and legs.

'You can get up, dear, it's all over. Now do your things up, kiss me, and go to bed.'

Gladys obeyed and with trembling hands tried to do up her knickers, but she was shaking so with sobs that she could not do it.

'There, dear, there, it's all over, I'm sorry I had to do it, but you won't bear me any malice, I'm sure, and you'll thank me in after-life, I know. Come, I've forgiven your fault, kiss and be friends.' She took the shrinking girl in her arms and petted her. Gladys flung her arms round her neck and buried her face on her shoulder.

'Oh, Auntie, it's the shame, the shame; the pain was bad enough, but, oh, the shame!'

'Silly little baby, what if Uncle Cecil had been present?'

'Oh don't.'

'Well, if you are very naughty, I shall know how to punish you, so don't give me any excuse. Now run along to bed and sleep well; I expect Uncle Cecil is tired of waiting about.'

'Oh, you don't think he heard, do you?' She cast a hurried, frightened look at the door and the window, but I dropped the blind just in time.

'No, silly,' said Muriel. 'Run along to bed. Shall I tell him he may come and say good-night to you? Or would you rather he didn't see you tonight?'

'I think I'd like to say good-night, but in the dark, please.'

'All right, baby, I'll tell him; now run along.' I heard a long kiss, and then after a minute, the front door opened, a shaft of light shone out, and Muriel whispered, 'You can come in.' I was surprised, for I didn't know she knew I was so near. I must have shown this on my face, for when I came in she said, 'You naughty boy, I saw the blind move. Come along in; I want you.'

❦ 4 ❦

Enlightenment

I was on fire. 'Wasn't it lovely?' said Muriel as I came into the room, and she flung herself in my arms. 'How much did you see?'

'Only Gladys. I didn't think of the blind in time for Ethel. Perhaps it's as well, for Gladys might have noticed me.'

'Never mind; next time there won't be any need for concealment, I fancy, if things go right. There won't be any difficulty about Ethel, I'm sure; she's ready for anything, but Gladys is more modest by nature. As you heard, it's the shame with her more than the pain.'

'We'll see what happens later tonight,' I said. 'I heard I was to say good-night. Give me half an hour and then you can come in and do what you like.'

'But it's too early for that yet; they'd think it funny if we went to bed so early. Besides we both want you here, and I'm sure you want us.' Her cunning hand sought my sex at once, which she found quite eager.

'One moment, that reminds me; you took that liberty once before with me today and I promised to whip you for it; come along, get ready.'

She pouted. 'Well, only a little one, I don't really deserve it; look at the good time I'm giving you, and I'm not at all jealous . . . still, I love you, darling, and you are going to let me whip you tonight, aren't you? . . . So come along, Juliette, my lord shall have his slaves to wait on him.' She began to undress and Juliette imitated her. I sat and watched them strip with gloating eyes. When they were both naked to their stockings, I took a birch, and, telling Juliette to hold Muriel, I began to whip the latter's plump cheeks. I did not want to hurt her, so I simply tickled her behind with the twigs, letting them curl here and there between the cheeks and legs. Now and then I gave a more vicious cut than usual, which provoked little hissing sighs from Muriel, but I did not set out to make her cry out, for we did not want the girls to hear. Still, the continual irritation of the blows fired her already heated blood and at last she began to plunge and heave, opening and contracting her legs. 'Harder, darling, harder, that's it – just between the legs; now, just between the cheeks . . . harder, now, now, now!' I followed her behests, and my eyes were greeted with visible proof of the pleasure she received. She disengaged herself from Juliette and, turning round, undid my trousers and, taking out the jewel she coveted, knelt down and began to devour it with kisses.

'Would you like a whipping too, Juliette?'

'You know I would; I love you whipping me, make me come too!'

'Bend over Muriel's back then. Muriel, get on your hands and knees.'

I sat down on a chair, so that Muriel could reach me kneeling between my legs. Juliette bent down across her naked back with her face towards my left hand, so that her bottom was just at the right angle for the rod. I plied it carefully and daintily, Muriel's tongue kept busy, the final paroxysm approached both for Juliette and myself, and as the supreme throbs shook my whole being, I succeeded in consummating Juliette's happiness as well. To make sure, I placed my fingers where the rod had caressed and was welcomed with tender contractions of the lips, and a copious flood of love.

'Now I'll go and wash and we'll have supper. You needn't dress if you don't want to.' I went to the door and turned the handle. As I was opening it, I heard the light pattering of feet up the stairs. I was just going to call the others, but thought better of it. They had noticed nothing, but were busy gathering up their clothes. I would keep that knowledge to myself, I thought; so I said nothing but went up to my room, washed, and came down again as if nothing had happened. We had supper and soon after we went to bed. Muriel's last words to me were: 'Now mind, there must be no taking of maidenheads. That is sacred. Anything else you like, and I will give you half an hour.'

I went to my room and undressed, and then in my pyjamas I went softly to the girls' room. My bedroom was really in the other cottage, but a 'pass-door' had been knocked through the party wall, both upstairs and down, so that the two cottages had become one house. I opened their door.

'Who's there?'

'May I come in? Muriel said you wanted me to say good-night to you.'

'Oh yes, come in, Uncle Cecil!'

I sat down on the chair by the side of the bed. A rising moon made the room not quite dark. I could see faintly the girlish faces under the bedclothes. I bent down and kissed the soft faces. Gladys's cheeks were still wet with tears, but Ethel's skin was burning. Her eyes shone bright in the gloom. 'Well, you poor babies, was it so very terrible?'

'Oh, Uncle, it was awful!' said Gladys, flinging her arms around me. I petted and consoled her and, slipping my hand under the clothes, stroked her still-burning bottom. She made no resistance, but snuggled closer to me. 'Here, that's not fair!' said Ethel, 'you've got him all, Gladys. Uncle Cecil, get in between us – you don't mind, Gladys, do you? I want him just as badly as you do, I got a much worse whipping than you.'

'Did you though?'

'Yes, look!' and she jumped out of bed and, in spite of Gladys's whispered remonstrance, lit the candle; then, pulling up her nightdress, she showed her little behind all scored with red. 'Gladys hasn't got half so many marks.' Before her sister could stop her, she pulled the clothes down and showed all her slim young form. Gladys uttered a little protest and buried her face in my lap. I gazed in rapture at the delicate curves. She was beautifully moulded. Just a few silky tendrils showed themselves on her virgin mount, but everywhere else the satin skin shone white and unblemished. The cheeks were slightly marked but nothing to speak of. Muriel, as I knew, had restrained herself. I couldn't resist it; I bent down and kissed both lovely cheeks. Instantaneously a pink flood spread over the skin – a beautiful blush. 'Oh, kiss mine too, and make it well,' whispered Ethel, flinging herself face downwards on my lap. I lifted the little nightdress and did as she asked. 'Darling Uncle Cecil, now lie down between us, and cuddle us.' I took her at her word, Gladys raising no objection. They snuggled up close to me, twining their arms round my neck and smothering my face with their sweet innocent kisses.

Ethel's entire body was burning hot. She was evidently of a much more passionate nature than her sister. It was more than flesh and blood could stand. My hands crept down until I found what I wanted – on my right the soft silky tendrils of Gladys's little pouting mount, and on my left the smooth tight lips of Ethel's narrow little pussy. The former took the caress quite discreetly. She sighed softly, but except for opening her thighs, did not show by any movement that she noticed my boldness. Ethel on the other hand clasped me tighter, spread her legs wide apart so that her left leg lay right over me. She even whispered in my ear, 'Oh, I love to feel your hand there; try and make me come, I never have yet. The girls at school have not been able to. Do try, Uncle.' I certainly couldn't resist the request and while Gladys's sighs came quicker and quicker and her soft thighs contracted nervously, Ethel suddenly said, 'Oh, something's going to happen, I feel so funny . . . tickle me harder, Uncle darling, oh . . . oh . . . ah.' She wriggled and twisted, and at last fell flat on me and I felt my fingers wet with her first sweet tribute to Venus. 'Oh, Uncle, Uncle, how lovely, how lovely!' I pressed my lips on hers in a long passionate kiss and, taking Gladys's hand, put it inside my pyjamas. She gave a little gasp when she found what I wanted her to find, but held it gently and caressingly.

'Uncle!' said Ethel suddenly, 'I want to ask you something. What were you doing downstairs, just before supper?'

'Oh, it was *you* I heard run upstairs, was it?'

'Yes, I thought I heard somebody being whipped, and crept down. Gladys was too frightened to, but I wanted to know, so I crept down and tried to peep through the keyhole.'

'Well, what did you see?'

'Nothing, the key was in the lock, but I'm sure somebody was being whipped, though it didn't sound like a cane. What was it?'

'I'll tell you tomorrow; I must go to bed now, or your auntie will be angry; you must go to sleep. Kiss me good-night, both of you.' I took them both in my arms and our lips met in a long loving embrace. We were still holding each other tightly when, as I was expecting, the door opened and Muriel and Juliette appeared with candles in their hands.

'What's the meaning of this?' she said, as she put the candles down on the chest of drawers.

'I was only saying good-night.'

'Indeed!' She came to the bed and before either of the girls could stop her – I, of course, made no attempt at resistance – pulled all the bedclothes off and laid bare all our naked bodies. Gladys's and Ethel's nightdresses were right up under their arms, my pyjama trousers were halfway down my thighs. At the sound of her aunt's voice Gladys had hidden her face in my shoulder and lay silent and trembling; Ethel had sat up with a start and faced Muriel, looking at her, half-boldly, half-nervously.

'I'm afraid you've caught us fairly, Muriel,' I said.

'Caught you fairly! Yes, and you'll catch it fairly, all of you. What have you done to these two? If it's anything irreparable you shall pay for it.'

'Oh no, there's no harm done.'

'I'll see for myself. Turn over, Gladys.' She pulled the girl's legs apart and pretended to investigate, then did the same for Ethel. 'Hm, you seem to have stopped in time, but you have evidently been grossly indecent. Juliette, fetch the cases quickly. I must whip these indecent games out of these girls' bottoms. As for you' – turning to me – 'I don't quite know how to treat you. If I treated you as the man you are, I should send you away at once, but that would probably make a scandal; if I treat you as a boy . . .'

Ethel broke in, 'Oh, don't send Uncle Cecil away, Auntie. It will be horrid without him.'

'You be quiet, Miss, if you want anything left of your bottom.'

'Treat me as you do them,' I said. 'I won't resist; and you see there is no real harm done.'

Muriel pretended to hesitate. Ethel whispered to me, 'But Auntie's going to whip us; do you mean you'll let her whip you?' I nodded. 'Oh, you *are* kind; I shan't mind being whipped so much if you are there and are being whipped too.'

Juliette had brought back the cases by this time.

'Get out of bed, all three of you,' ordered Muriel, 'and stand by the side with your backs to me. Gladys, you here at the top; Cecil, you next; and you, Ethel, here. Now bend forward as far as you can. Juliette, turn up those nightdresses.' As Juliette took hold of Gladys's nightdress, I felt a tremor run through her body and her hand sought and found mine. I held it tightly during all the punishment. Since Muriel's entrance, she had not uttered a word. Ethel did not wait for Juliette's help; she pulled her own nightdress right up to her armpits and bent forward. 'Is that right, Auntie?' she had the temerity to say.

'You seem in a great hurry,' said Muriel. 'You won't be quite so eager before it's over.'

'If I've got to be whipped, I've got to be whipped,' said Ethel philosophically. 'The sooner we begin the better. Ow! I didn't know you were ready,' as Muriel's hand fell with a resounding smack on her bottom.

Then this threefold whipping began. Muriel admitted afterwards to me, it was the finest time she had ever had. She used the back of a hairbrush first, and then when she had reddened our cheeks enough to suit her, she took the birch. When the first cut from this fell on Gladys, she gave a little cry – the first sound she had uttered – and clutched my hand convulsively. Ethel looked up at the noise just as I received my dose. 'Oh, so that was it,' I heard her say to herself. 'Oh! Oh!' she cried out loud as her bottom felt for the first time the tingling twigs. She wriggled and squirmed, and tried to cover her cheeks with her hands.

'Juliette, tie Ethel's hands together, or better still, Cecil, you hold them.'

'Better not resist,' I whispered to Ethel.

'I don't mind with you here,' she whispered back. 'I know now; golly! but it does hurt!'

'One, two, three,' the blows fell rhythmetically on each of our devoted behinds. To me, of course, the whipping was not half as severe as the others I had received at Muriel's hands. Besides, the thought of those two young bottoms, one on either side of me, as naked as my own, fired my imagination and whetted my desires. I could feel Gladys's hand clutch mine convulsively every time a blow fell, sobs shook her whole body, but shame seemed to have paralysed her entirely and she lay practically motionless, accepting her punishment in a kind of dull stupor. Ethel, on the other hand, twisted and wriggled and cried out with the pain of each blow. Shame seemed to play but a small part with her.

But the birch was becoming worn-out, and Muriel was evidently tiring. 'We must finish,' she said. 'Stand up.' We obeyed her. 'Juliette, take Ethel on your back, and Cecil, you take Gladys. Take their legs under your arms.' Gladys shivered with apprehension as she clasped her arms round my neck, and Muriel lifted each leg under my arms.

'Haven't we had enough?' said Ethel. 'I'm sure my bottom's cut to pieces. You *are* cruel, Auntie!'

'Be quiet,' said Muriel. I had thought she was going to use the cane, or a fresh birch, but from the sound of the first blow on Gladys, followed quickly by one on my own loins, I realised it was the whip of knotted cords that she had chosen. The first cut curled right round between Gladys's legs, which were stretched wide apart. She shrieked in surprise and pain. 'Oh, Auntie, please, not there ... I can't bear that ... oh mercy, mercy.' She tried to free her legs, but I held them tightly.

'Ah, I thought you would find your tongue before I had done with you. Yes, I thought so,' as another cut fell, producing a still more piercing cry. 'The whip isn't quite so nice as Uncle Cecil's fingers, I expect, but it's better for you ... Now, Miss Ethel, how do *you* like it?'

She turned to the sister and the little lashes curled wickedly in between the slim legs. 'Oh, you beast, you cat!' screamed Ethel. 'Oh, oh, oh, you'll kill me, let me go.' She twisted and writhed so violently that she managed to get one leg free from Juliette's grasp and stood down on it – the other leg was still caught up – hopping about to avoid the blows.

'Careful, Muriel,' I whispered.

'It's not fair to whip one there,' sobbed Ethel. '*You* wouldn't like it. Ooh! You've made me bleed!' as she looked at her hand, which she had pressed to the injured part.

'Let her go, Juliette, let me see.' She drew the angry, shrinking girl to her and placed her finger tenderly between her legs. The lash had just cut the skin of one of the tender lips. 'I'm sorry, I didn't mean to do that, dear. It's not much. Juliette, get some ointment, we mustn't spoil the pretty little jewel. There, baby, there, Auntie is sorry, let me make it well.' She drew Ethel on to her knee, and went on caressing the tender slit. Under her clever, cunning fingers the girl let herself go and suddenly flung her arms round Muriel's neck and kissed her, while I saw her little bottom wriggle and the thighs contract and imprison Muriel's hand.

'There, is that better?'

'Ye–es, but that was what Uncle Cecil did, and you whipped us for it. You ought to be whipped too.'

'Uncle and I are different, you naughty creature.'

'Of course you are, I know that . . . '

'What are you doing – who told you, you might put your hand there?'

While this had been going on I had lifted Gladys on to the bed and laid her tenderly down. She clung to me and kissed me between her sobs. She had carefully pulled her nightdress down and I respected her wishes and kept my hand from wandering. When I heard Muriel say those last words, I looked round just in time to see Ethel's hand disappear in the folds of Muriel's dressing-gown. Muriel caught my eye. 'Here's a naughty girl,' she said to me. 'What is one to do with her? . . . Ethel, Ethel, don't. Oh, you little devil, who taught you to do that?'

'Gladys and the other girls at school; they say my fingers are nicer than anyone's, are they?' I saw the busy arm working. Muriel was fast becoming beside herself with passion. Ethel was taking her back to her schooldays. Her eyes half-closed, the pupils were turned right up. She lay back panting. I was in agony. I dared not do what I wanted to Gladys, for if I began I knew not where I should end, and I had promised Muriel to respect her virginity and intended to keep my promise. In despair I took Gladys's hand and placed it round my eager, swollen engine. Then taking her by the wrist I moved it up and down. She opened her eyes when she felt John Thomas in her hand and smiled lovingly at me. Then she pulled up her nightdress, blushing most adorably, and, taking my hand from her wrist, placed it on her mount. She went on working her own hand, however, and I felt the supreme moment approaching.

At this moment Juliette came back. 'I can't find the ointment, Muriel . . . ' she began. 'Why, here's a happy party! But where do I come in?'

'Juliette,' I gasped, 'come here, I've got something for you. Quick, quick . . . ' She ran to me and, kneeling down, was just in time to receive all the force of my pent-up passion.

❧ 5 ❧

An Objectionable Bathing Costume

The next morning I woke quite early, about seven o'clock. The sun had climbed over the hills behind Croyde. I put on my bathing suit and a dressing-gown and went to call the others. I went into the girls' room first and found them fast asleep in each other's arms. Gladys's nightdress was undone, and Ethel's dark head rested on her sister's breast. They made a lovely picture. I very gently pulled the clothes down and saw that each had her hand on the other's sex. I bent down and kissed them. Ethel opened her eyes, saw me, and jumped out of bed to throw herself into my arms. Gladys started and, half-awake, said, 'Oh, no more whipping, please, Auntie!' Then she saw me, pulled her nightdress down, and held out her arms, smiling up at me. 'Oh, it's you, Uncle Cecil, I was afraid . . . ' She did not finish the sentence.

'Come out and bathe, it's a lovely day.'

'I'm so tired and sore,' she murmured.

'A bathe will do you all the good in the world. Hurry up and put your things on. I'll go and call the others.'

Gladys stretched herself and yawned; Ethel was already getting into her costume.

'Oh bother, all the buttons are off mine; I meant to sew them on yesterday,' said Gladys. 'I forgot.' She blushed rosy red at the remembrance of what had driven it from her mind.

'Never mind that, there'll be no one about.'

'Don't let's wear any at all,' said Ethel. 'It will be much jollier bathing naked. Uncle Cecil won't mind, and I don't mind him.'

'What will your auntie say?'

'Oh lor! I suppose she'd make that an excuse for another whipping. I want to talk to you, Uncle Cecil, about her; she seems very fond of whipping.'

'I must go and call her, you can talk to me later.' I went to Muriel's room and found her and Juliette in the same attitude as I had found Gladys and Ethel. I pulled the clothes down quickly and smacked both their naked bottoms.

'You beast, Cecil,' said Muriel, sitting up.

'Come and bathe,' I said.

'No, I'm too tired. I'll bathe after breakfast.'

'Well, the girls are coming.'

'All right, you go with them. Breakfast at nine. Leave me and Juliette here.'

I didn't press her but went back to the others. They were waiting in their mackintoshes. Gladys had pinned her costume together, but the fastening was very frail. 'Muriel and Juliette are too tired to get up.'

'Hurrah!' said Ethel. 'We'll have some fun, come on,' and she danced down the beach. We put the mackintoshes in a safe place out of reach of the tide, and plunged into the breakers. At the first stroke Gladys's frail fastening parted, and her dress gaped wide open.

'Oh, dear,' she said, looking at me.

'Take it off, Gladys, I'll take mine off,' said Ethel, 'and Uncle Cecil, you'll take yours off too, won't you?'

I hesitated, for it seemed quite a different thing to expose oneself in cold blood to two practically innocent girls, and to let them see, and handle, a member that was in fighting trim. But Ethel didn't wait. She skipped out of the water and hurriedly unbuttoned her dress, pulled it off her shoulders, and then stepped out of the legs. 'Come on, Gladys, come on, Uncle Cecil, play fair.'

'Shall I?' said Gladys.

'There's no one to see; it won't matter.' I took hold of her dress and took it off; then I wriggled out of my own, and we all three stood naked in the morning sun.

'How I hate clothes,' said Ethel. 'Don't you, Uncle Cecil? . . . Oh look, Gladys, Uncle Cecil's quite different from how he was last night. There's nothing left of him.'

I felt absurdly self-conscious at this remark, but John Thomas evidently either liked attention being drawn to him or was eager to assert his importance, for I felt him swell appreciably.

'Oh look, its growing bigger. Oh, how funny.' She came to me and touched it.

'Ethel, for shame,' said Gladys, 'out in the open air; come into the water; suppose Auntie saw you.'

'Oh lor!' said Ethel with a quick look at the cottage, and she rushed into the sea. We romped about for some time, but it was too cold at that time of the morning to stay in long, and soon we were running back to the house. I was dressed long before breakfast and so was Ethel. She came down and found me smoking a cigarette in a deck-chair in front of the cottage. She sprang on to my knee and cuddled up to me.

'Feeling better for the bathe?'

'Yes, but the salt water did make my bottom smart. Gladys is upstairs putting cold cream on hers . . . Uncle Cecil, do tell me, who was getting whipped last night before supper? I know someone was and with a bundle of those twigs that Auntie used on us.'

'A birch,' I said.

'Oh, is *that* a birch? Who was getting it? Juliette?'

'Yes, and Muriel.'

'Auntie! Oh, who was whipping her?

'I was.'

'Oh, I wish I could have seen that. But why? Did she let you? Tell me.' She wriggled about in her precocious naughtiness.

'She had been naughty to me, so I whipped her just as she whipped you.'

'Ooh . . . but Uncle, she whipped us for doing that – you know; and she did just the same to me and let me do it to her; she liked it too, I know. I don't think it's fair. If we deserved whipping so does she.'

'Tell her so.'

'Oh, I dare say!'

'Shall I tell her what you think?'

'Oh no, she'd be angry and then . . . ' She rubbed herself behind suggestively.

Gladys came down at this moment. I held out my hand. She came and kissed me.

'So you've been putting on cold cream; is it very sore?' She blushed divinely and nodded her head.

'How do you know? Did Ethel . . . ? You little horror!'

'Breakfast!,' came Muriel's voice. She appeared in the door. 'Morning, girls, all right this morning?' Ethel ran to her quite frankly, but Gladys hung back shyly.

'Come, Gladys, don't be shy, last night's quite forgotten. That's better.' She took Gladys in her arms and kissed her fondly. 'You don't bear any grudge against your auntie, do you?'

'No, Auntie.'

'That's right, we shall be fonder of each other than ever, if I'm not mistaken.'

We went in to breakfast. Muriel was in the best of spirits, evidently very pleased with herself. The girls, Gladys especially, needed a little drawing out, but by the time the meal was over all constraint had vanished and we were the same merry party as yesterday. 'You'll bathe later, Muriel?' I said.

'Oh yes, about twelve o'clock. It will give me an appetite for dinner. What are you all going to do? Explore, or laze about and bathe with me?'

'Oh, it's too hot to do much,' I said. 'Eh! girls?'

'I must put the buttons on my costume,' said Gladys. 'Pins aren't any good,' she added with a roguish look at me.

'Would you like to wear yours all the morning, Ethel?' said Muriel. 'There doesn't seem to be anybody about.'

'May I?'

'Yes, if you like. Then you can get as wet as you like.'

Muriel was in so good a temper that I decided to make a suggestion to her which I thought promised much fun to myself. I bent forward and kissed her. 'They are sweet girls, aren't they?'

'Yes, perfect darlings – especially Ethel – oh what a delightful hand she has! Oh Cecil, wasn't it a glorious night! To see your three bottoms there waiting to be whipped. I can see them now – ' She closed her eyes in ecstasy. 'And then afterwards, Ethel's fingers. Do you know she got all four of them in, the little darling. I'd forgive her anything – no, I couldn't though, I must whip her little bottom again – but I wouldn't whip it hard. Oh, she's a darling.'

'Yes, but she doesn't think you're quite fair.'

'Eh, why not?'

'Well, she argues, quite logically, that you whipped us three for doing precisely what you did to her, and let her do to you; and you liked it, she said, she knew you did.'

'The little devil!'

'Isn't it true? . . . Now I've got an idea, let her whip you; tell her that it is quite true you deserve a whipping and she shall give it to you.'

'What, me let a slip of a girl whip me! Not much; it's all very well for you, but I'm not going to offer my bottom to her, thank you.'

'All right, just as you like; it's only a suggestion. I thought it might be amusing.'

'It would be to you perhaps.'

'You won't be angry with Ethel for saying what she did?'

'Oh no, I like her spirit . . . the little devil, she's a girl after my own heart – up to any devilment. But it doesn't mean that I'm going to let her whip me,' she added as she went away.

'I'll bet a quid,' I said to myself, 'that she *does* whip you before we leave here, if I connive at it.'

The girls came rushing downstairs and dragged me along with them to the beach. Ethel was wearing her bathing costume, as Muriel had told her she might, and looked the young imp she was. Gladys had on her blouse and skirt but, as she confided to me, had her bathing things on underneath. 'It's so much more comfortable,' she told me, 'than corsets and things.'

'And has the cold cream proved effective?' I asked, continuing the conversation which breakfast had interrupted. She nodded and blushed.

'Oh, Uncle, wasn't it awful. You know I'd never been whipped before yesterday. I thought I should have died of shame when Auntie came in and found us in bed. And she is cruel; but do you know, just towards the end, when I was on your back and she made the whip curl all in and out, I felt so funny, just as if things were going to happen – you know – just as if I was being tickled by you.'

'Ah, quite so, and didn't it happen?'

'Not then, she stopped too soon, and you put me in bed.'

'And then?'

'Then you know it did . . . But tell me, would it have happened if Auntie had gone on?'

'Probably.'

'Ooh!'

'Why, do you wish it had?'

'Ye–es . . . not with Auntie, but . . . ' – she threw herself into my arms – 'I think I'd like it to happen that way with you.'

I held her tight, my hand went round her thighs seeking her little pussy.

'Not that way, not from behind, I'm too sore.' She opened her legs, so that I could reach her from the front. Ethel had been busy paddling and playing in the sand while we had been talking, but now she saw what was going on. She ran up to us.

'Oh, you rude things, I'll tell Auntie,' and she began spanking her sister with her sandal. I got up and chased her, caught her, and turned her over. Then, taking the sandal from her, I belaboured her little behind, not too hard, but hard enough to be felt. She squealed and kicked, and at last managed to escape.

'You big bully!' she called out from a safe distance, rubbing her smarting hams.

The morning passed like this, until we saw Muriel and Juliette coming down the beach ready to bathe. I jumped up and, going behind a rock, got into my bathing suit. Gladys simply slipped off her blouse and skirt and was ready. We all plunged into the surf and romped about. We played the usual games, dodging the breakers, diving under them, dancing round in a ring, and so on. The sea was as smooth as it ever is on that coast, which meant that the waves were quite three or four feet high, and quite strong enough to take you off your feet if you weren't careful. I suggested a game of touch, and soon shrieks of excitement rose high. I noticed with glee that whenever Ethel was 'he' she always made a dead set at Muriel and once or twice, when she managed to catch her, smacked her as near the bottom as she dared. Muriel took it all in good part and retaliated. Once, when she was chasing Ethel in shallow water, a wave came and bowled her over. Muriel was on her in a moment and, under the pretence of helping her up, administered two or three smart slaps.

'That's not fair,' shouted Ethel, wriggling away. 'Only one smack's allowed, isn't it, Uncle Cecil?'

'Yes,' I said, 'let's pay her out; come on, Gladys and Juliette,' and I led the way in a chase of Muriel. She entered into the game and dodged here and there, but we were too quick for her and she fell on the soft sand with the rest of us on top of her, tickling and smacking her wherever we could. Ethel managed to get two or three resounding smacks on the plump thighs before our victim begged for mercy.

'That'll do,' she panted. 'Now, Cecil, it's your turn.'

I started at once and sped away, the rest of them shrieking in my pursuit. I dodged and doubled and at last let myself be caught by Juliette and Gladys, who fell on me and slapped me vigorously. The others came up and added their smacks, I rolled over and defended myself, but the blows followed me, and Muriel even dared to slap the obvious protrusion sticking out in front. I seized her hand and pulled her down across me, and administered a sound smacking on her kicking legs and cheeks.

'Cecil, you devil, stop, not before the girls.' The others had stood away when they saw Muriel in this position.

'Go on, Uncle Cecil, give it to her,' shouted Ethel, beside herself with excitement.

'Don't you be cheeky, youngster,' I said, 'or you'll be sorry . . . Juliette, catch her and show her respect for her elders.' Ethel shrieked and fled, but she couldn't escape Juliette, and in a trice she was across the latter's knee and was uttering little squeals under the quick-descending palm.

Our games and running about had tired us completely, and we were all ready for dinner. This morning's entertainment had also achieved one other result. It had taken away the last shred of modesty – mock or real – from all of us, and from that time on, there was no reticence or concealment on the part of any of us, not even Gladys.

✥ 6 ✥

Jealousy and an Apple-pie Bed

There was a lull for a day or two after these events. The girls – even Ethel – were on their best behaviour, and they seemed to get to know just how far they could go with Muriel. If she was in a reckless mood they fell in with it, if on the other hand she was not inclined for improprieties, they also were more sedate. Gladys had quite lost her shyness and evidently was growing very fond of me. This, I thought, did not altogether please Muriel. I noticed on more than one occasion looks, certainly not of love, and several times Muriel seemed to lay traps for Gladys so that she might have an occasion to punish her. But the girl managed to avoid pitfalls and the occasion never came – at any rate, for a considerable time. One evening, however, the weather was very heavy – thunder was in the air – our nerves were all on edge – and Ethel in particular was very restless and irritable. She *would* tease all of us – with Muriel and myself she restrained herself, realising that it might be the worse for her if she went too far – but Juliette and Gladys she never left alone for a minute. At last Gladys could stand it no longer – she wanted to read and Ethel would not leave her alone – so with a 'get out, you little beast,' she boxed her sister's ears. The force of the unexpected blow sent Ethel into the fender. She got up at once and went for Gladys and a rough-and-tumble ensued, during which a chair was broken.

Muriel and I were sitting outside smoking. Hearing the noise we came in just in time to save the table with the lighted lamp from going over and setting the place on fire. 'What's all this about?' asked Muriel.

'Gladys knocked me into the fireplace,' said Ethel.

'She wouldn't let me read.'

'That's no excuse for breaking the furniture and nearly setting the place on fire. Go upstairs, both of you, and undress, and come down again to me.' Gladys went out without a word, Ethel made a face at her aunt and followed her.

'Juliette, get the birches. You'll stop this time and watch, I suppose, Cecil?'

'Why shouldn't I help?'

'No, I and Juliette will be quite enough, and besides, you'd probably want to whip Gladys and that *I* mean to do.'

'Oh,' I said. 'Why?'

'Never mind why. It's enough that I *want* to. Juliette, aren't those girls ready? Go and see.'

Juliette went out and returned shepherding the two culprits. They were in their nightdresses only. Muriel assumed a most businesslike air. 'Juliette, will you take Ethel and whip her soundly; Gladys, turn your nightdress up and bend over the sofa as you did before.'

'But Auntie . . . Uncle Cecil.'

'Well, what about him? It's a little late to be bashful before him; come be quick, it will be worse for you if you keep me waiting.'

The poor girl began to pull up her things, blushing rosy red. 'Higher than that, right round your waist – that's better – now bend down, lower, lower still. That's it!' and the rod fell fairly across both cheeks.

Juliette had in the meantime managed to get Ethel across her knees, keeping her legs tight between her own and her head tucked under her left arm. She was using a shortish birch and the blows fell obliquely on the white skin. Ethel plunged and squealed but could not escape.

Whish – whish – whish! The blows were falling on poor Gladys. 'How dare you lose your temper with your sister!' Whish – whish! 'Perhaps you think because your Uncle Cecil makes a fuss of you, you are mistress here. I'll teach you.' Whish – whish – whish!

Then I realised the state of the case. Muriel was jealous. Though she had professed to be glad at our happy family freedom, she really was jealous of my evident attention to Gladys and her affection for me.

Gladys began to sob and moan under the blows.

'Yes, I dare say you'd rather have your uncle's caresses than mine. But it's my turn now, mine, mine, mine.' The birch came crashing down. Gladys's cries became more acute, quite drowning Ethel's squawls. I glanced over at her; Juliette had given her a good warming and her bottom was all crimson. She caught my eye and I signed to her to stop. Ethel got off her knee and clapped her hands to her burning cheeks. She then jumped on a chair and, through her tears, tried to look at herself in the glass.

'My word, but you have laid it on, Juliette,' she said, 'but I'm glad I had you and not Auntie. Ooh, look at Gladys's behind.'

Muriel was still bringing the birch pitilessly down on her victim, holding her down with her left hand.

Gladys's cries were pitiful to hear. Muriel seemed beside herself. I thought it time to interfere.

'That's enough, Muriel,' I said.

'You be quiet,' she answered and the blows fell again.

I stepped forward and seized her arm. 'Let me go!' she shouted, but I held her tight.

'Gladys and Ethel, go upstairs,' I said, 'and go to bed, I'll come and say good-night later.' Gladys got up and stumbled sobbing out of the room. Ethel followed her, looking rather frightened.

When they were gone, I released Muriel and shut the door. Then I turned to her. 'Now Muriel,' I said, 'what's the meaning of this? How dare you lose your temper and flog Gladys so unmercifully?'

'I'd like to kill her,' she gasped in angry sobs. She was shaking with passion.

'Why?' And then it all came out. I was always with her; I loved Gladys better than I did her. She wasn't going to play second fiddle to any little chit of a girl, I was cruel and unkind, I was everything that was bad, and so on.

I kept quite cool. 'Now Muriel, this has got to stop, here and now. There's no reason for you to be jealous at all and I won't have it. You told Gladys just now that you were mistress here, now I'm going to show you that I am master. Take off your things, and kneel down and ask me to punish you as you deserve.'

'I won't, I won't be whipped.'

'Oh won't you, we'll see about that, now down on your knees.' She glared at me, shaking with anger. I went towards her. She put up her arms to protect her face. But I seized her by the shoulders and shook her till her teeth rattled and her hair came tumbling down. This mode of treatment was evidently new to her, and most effectual. 'Oh, let me go, I *will* do what you want.'

'Kneel down.'

She knelt down.

'Now say, "I beg your pardon, Cecil, for being jealous and losing my temper, and I deserve to be punished, please punish me as I deserve." ' She repeated the words after me. 'Now undress.' She began fumbling at her things. 'Help her, Juliette.' With Juliette's aid she soon stood naked to her stockings. 'Now bring me a birch and ask me to use it.' She did as I told her. 'Now, Juliette, hold her under your arm.'

'Oh Cecil, dear, not too hard.' My reply was a long drawing cut right across her loins; she sobbed and writhed. Blow followed blow. I had no intention of sparing her, for I was really very angry. The birch soon was used up.

'Juliette, get me a riding whip.' Juliette released her to do as I said. Muriel fell on her knees and clasped my legs.

'Oh, not the whip, Cecil, not the whip, please.'

'Well, will you promise to be good and beg Gladys's pardon if I let you off?'

'Yes, oh yes.'

I called up the stairs, 'Juliette, bring Gladys down with you.'

Gladys appeared, looking very frightened; poor thing, she evidently thought the whip was for her. She stared wide-eyed when she saw Muriel naked at my feet. 'Now Muriel,' I said, 'do as you promised.' She did not move, her pride would not let her turn and face her victim of half an hour ago. I took the whip from Juliette and made it whistle through the air. She shuddered but still did not move. I brought it down diagonally across her bottom and thighs. She leapt up and sprang towards Gladys. The latter started back in fright.

'Oh Gladys, don't let him whip me any more, don't let him.' Gladys looked at me in a puzzled way.

'I have been whipping Muriel,' I said, 'because she lost her temper with you through jealousy, when she has no reason. I have told her to beg your pardon.'

'Yes, I do, I do Gladys,' sobbed Muriel at the girl's feet. 'I'm sorry, please forgive me and ask him not to whip me any more.'

It was a supreme delight to me to see this proud woman humbling herself at the feet of a mere girl. I gazed to my fill on the scene, but Gladys evidently felt uncomfortable.

'Auntie dear, get up, don't kneel like that to me; of course I forgive you. I was naughty I know, and I dare say I *did* deserve a whipping, though perhaps not such a hard one. But you needn't be jealous of me. I'm only a girl, and I'm sure Uncle Cecil is as fond of us all, without any favourites.' She drew the older woman up as she spoke, and held her in her arms. 'There,' she went on, 'go to him now – goodnight, Uncle Cecil – no, I'll say good-night here – you see Auntie Muriel to bed, I expect Ethel is wondering what is happening to me.'

I was surprised at her cleverness. She led her aunt to me, kissed us both long and lovingly, and went out.

Muriel fell into my arms, and I followed Gladys's advice. In fact my own bed did not see me at all that night.

The next morning I did not wake up as early as usual, which was not to be wondered at, considering all the circumstances. The sun was well up when I opened my eyes and found Muriel beside me, with her arms round my neck.

She opened her eyes as I moved.

'Are you getting up?'

'Yes, it's past eight. I must go and call the girls, or we shall lose our morning swim.'

'Send Gladys to me, I want her . . . you needn't look like that, I'm not jealous any longer, I want to tell her so, and make her love me.'

I went into the girls' room. Ethel was awake, but Gladys was still asleep. 'I was wondering when you were coming,' said the former. 'Didn't you sleep well last night?' She said this with such a meaning air that I thought Gladys must have given her a hint as to where I spent the night.

'Oh yes,' I replied innocently. 'Why do you ask?'

'Oh nothing; here, wake up, Gladys, here's Uncle Cecil.' And she pulled the clothes down and began to tickle her sister between the legs.

Gladys moved restlessly and murmured half-asleep, 'No, don't, I'm too tired.' Then she opened her eyes and saw me. She hastily pulled her nightdress down and tried to gather up bedclothes. 'Oh, Ethel, you *are* rude.'

'Your auntie wants you,' I said. 'Oh, you needn't look so frightened, she's quite all right this morning; run along to her. Shall we go for a swim, Ethel?'

'Rather,' and she hopped out of bed at once and, without waiting for me to go, pulled off her nightdress and stook stark naked looking at her bathing dress.

'Ethel!' said Gladys. 'I'd be ashamed.'

'Who cares for Uncle Cecil?' laughed Ethel, as I went to my own room and Gladys went to find Muriel.

When I reached my own room and began to untidy the bed so that Mrs Tasker should not discover that it had not been slept in, I discovered why Ethel had been so anxious to know how I slept. That favourite practical joke of the schoolgirl – an apple-pie bed – met my eyes. Without pausing to think how I was giving the whole show away, I rushed back to Ethel. 'You little devil, I know now why you asked so particularly how I slept last night. I'll teach you to make apple-pie beds.' She was half in and half out of her bathing dress.

'Hullo! only just found it out?' She shouted with laughter as she dodged me. 'Who were you with last night?'

I seized hold of her and threw her, laughing, on the bed, tearing off the dress; she kicked and squirmed and squealed as I tickled her all over, trying to lay her across my knees. Her struggles revealed all she had to show, my eager fingers probed every secret access, my gloating eyes followed my fingers. She tried her best to retaliate, and in the struggle the girdle of my pajamas came undone and the loose trousers fell down over my thighs. Instinctively her hand fastened round the pendulous engine that was revealed. His night's labours with Muriel had left him rather limp, but under the exciting touch of Ethel's fingers he did his best to assert himself and make a brave show.

'What a funny thing this is,' said Ethel. I had stopped tickling her when her fingers began this present task. 'It's never twice alike. When I first saw it, it was quite stiff and hard and long, and then when we were bathing yesterday, it had shrunk to nearly nothing – now it's bigger again, but quite flabby; and what are those two little round things for in that rough bag? . . . Oh, it's getting bigger again and stiff . . . Am I making it do that, by rubbing it?'

'Yes, you darling, go on rubbing it up and down – and hold it tight . . . oh, not so tight as that . . . that's better, draw the skin right back – now up again.'

'Oh, Uncle, look, it's all messy – don't you want to go somewhere?'

'No, no, go on rubbing, quicker, quicker,' and my hand searched between her legs.

'Oh, the horrid thing, it's spitting at me again . . . it's all over my leg . . . oh, Uncle darling, I'm coming, I'm coming.'

We were sitting side by side on the bed, and in her final paroxysm, her head fell forward nearly on to my lap. Naturally, she received the final bursts on her face. But she was too overcome to notice it. I pressed her gently down until her face met the rampant head. She seemed instinctively to know what I wanted and, opening her lips, kissed and sucked the now declining knob. When she had quite drained me, I raised her face to mine and pressed loving kisses on her lips, heedless of the fact that they were still wet with my own strength. She clung to me for a minute or two and then, sitting up, looked at her thighs. 'You *have* made me in a mess. What is that sticky stuff – it does taste funny. Oh look, there are little bits of jelly in it. What's that?'

'Those are babies.'

'Oh, what a lot! But how? I don't understand.'

'Well, you see, if I were to push this into you there, and rub it up and down inside you, just as you rubbed it up and down with your hand, that stuff would come out of me and mix with you when you came, and might give you a baby.'

'Oh I see, but you could never get that in here.' She opened her legs and pulled her slit open, showing the dainty inner lips all wet and glistening still.

'You're a naughty girl,' I said, 'and you deserve a whipping; I haven't whipped you yet for making me an apple-pie bed.'

'How was it you didn't find it out until just now? Where were you? – oh not too hard! please – I know, with Auntie Muriel! What were you doing to her, what you've just shown me? – you can do it harder than that if you like – will she have a baby?'

'Don't be so inquisitive! She won't have any babies, I can tell you that . . . Come on, let's go and bathe.'

'Oh, those last three hurt. Where's Gladys? Isn't she coming? Let's go and find her.'

Before I could stop her, she had run out of the room. I followed her, for I was eager to see what was happening. I caught her up before she reached the door, which was open, and went in with her. What a picture met my eyes! At first sight it was difficult to distinguish the two forms, so interlaced were the limbs. But after a moment I realised what was happening. Held tightly between Muriel's thighs was Gladys's fair head – I could not see her face, that was hidden; her beautiful bottom was well exposed, showing the traces of last night's punishment, and just beyond that I could see Muriel's forehead and abundant tresses.

'Well I never!' I laughed. 'Is that how you make friends?'

At the sound of my voice, Gladys started up, wrenched herself away from Muriel's grasp, and tried to bury herself in the clothes. She seemed to blush all over, for a pink flush flooded all her skin. Muriel looked towards me with satisfaction in her eyes. 'You might have waited a moment, Cecil. . . . Hullo! is that Ethel? Well, that's a nice costume to come and say good-morning to one's aunt in, how dare you? come here.' She drew the girl, who was all eyes, close to her, patting her bottom in mock severity. 'Why, what's this? Cecil, you haven't . . . ' Her tone became quite severe.

'Oh, it's all right,' I hastened to reassure her, 'something got spilt.'

'Did it? Well, you've interrupted us, so you had better help us to finish. I'm going to kiss this little witch now though. She can kiss you; I expect she knows how to by this time; as a treat you can kiss Gladys – come out of those clothes – and she can go on kissing me. Now, Ethel, lie across the top of the bed – you, Cecil, down that side – Gladys, you across the bottom, can you reach me? Open your legs a little wider, Ethel. That's it, ahh!' The result of this magic circle or square may be imagined. Anyhow, we forgot all about breakfast-time. While we were in the height of our enjoyment, Juliette appeared in the doorway. I was too busy between Gladys's soft thighs to say anything to her. She went out again, and I thought that she had gone away not wishing to interrupt. To my surprise she came back in a minute holding something behind her back.

'Well, that's a pretty sight,' she laughed. 'It's far too good an opportunity to be lost though.' With that she produced the birch which she had hidden and brought it lightly down on Ethel's and Gladys's thighs. They sprang up, startled, and jumped off the bed, leaving Muriel and myself exposed. 'For shame, you two,' she went on, 'get up and dress,' and she playfully flicked me between the thighs and caressed Muriel's mount.

'I suppose we had better,' said Muriel, sitting up. 'We mustn't over-tire ourselves. Run along, girls, and dress. Breakfast in a quarter of an hour. We'll play this game again sometime if you're good.'

'Yes, but I want to take a hand then,' said Juliette, 'it's mean of you to have left me out this time.'

Things went on smoothly for some days after this. Muriel had forgotten her jealousy and had had enough whipping for the time being. I also was not disinclined for a little respite and time for recuperation. The open-air lazy life, however, coupled with the sea-bathing, acted as a splendid tonic, and before many days passed I was fit and ready for anything. Juliette also was eager to take a hand, as she called it, in the 'circle', which on this occasion became what Euclid might have called an irregular pentagon. This time, however, the order was reversed, and I tasted the virgin sweets of Ethel's smooth young body, while her sister caressed me. Muriel lay between Gladys and Juliette while the latter's body squirmed under Ethel's clever, insinuating little tongue.

How long we lay in these mutual embraces, I could not say, but naturally I tired before any of the girls, and when I realised that I was for the time being milked dry, I began to cast about in my mind for some other variations. I got up and, whispering to Gladys to join herself to her sister for the time being, left the happy party. I had determined what I would do. I found a candle on the dressing-table and, going round to the other side of the bed, found Muriel's soft cheeks and, signing to Juliette not to say anything or to stop her own busy tongue, inserted it gently between them. Muriel stopped and looked round.

'What's that? . . . Cecil, you devil!'

I pushed it further in. 'Oh, oh . . . no, don't stop; only go carefully, don't hurt me, ah! that's it . . . oh, how lovely!' The intensity of her pleasure as I worked the candle in and out made her now fierce in her passion, so that she tried to draw all Gladys's tender little pussy into her mouth, draining its juice and sucking it with fierce-sounding smacks of her lips. She was also evidently using her teeth, for I heard Gladys sigh, 'Oh, Auntie, don't bite me!' Then I saw her hands clutch at Ethel's little bottom and pinch the cheeks, while Ethel in her turn fiercely devoured Juliette. I watched this wave of passion circulate through the four bodies, while I made good use of the candle. At last Muriel's head fell away from Gladys and she sighed, 'I'm *done*, I can't do any more . . . Cecil . . . Juliette, stop for God's sake you'll kill me.' The two girls sat up and watched us three others, Ethel staring with huge eyes at my treatment of Muriel, who was twisting and writhing in the last throes of passion. Her face was white, her eyes half-closed, her breath came in gasps, her fingers clutched and opened convulsively, great drops of perspiration stood on her forehead. Her belly heaved and fell, her loins worked forward and back as her thighs pressed on Juliette's head and then again relaxed. At last she seemed to pull herself together for a supreme effort, held herself rigid for a moment or two, and then collapsed supine, motionless, inert.

ও 7 ঙ

The Day Trip

One morning on waking we found the sea very rough. A sou'-wester had sprung up during the night, and great breakers came rolling into the bay; far out, white-horses could be seen everywhere, and Lundy looked suspiciously clear and near. We had our morning swim – or rather bathe, for it was far too rough to attempt swimming. Indeed, the force of the waves was so great that it was difficult to keep one's footing. Ethel in fact gave it up as a bad job. Every time a roller came in, it carried her with it on to the beach, where she needed all her strength to prevent herself being sucked back by the undertow. Her legs and arms flew in all directions. It was exciting and tiring work. At last a wave broke suddenly right across Muriel's back. She shrieked and made for the shore. She told me afterwards it felt just like a cut from a riding whip; indeed, there was a red weal right across her shoulders which might well have been made in that way. 'I'm sick of the sea,' she said at breakfast. 'Let's go inland today.'

We accordingly packed luncheon baskets, hired the pony and jingle which had brought us from Morthoe and which belonged to a man in the village, and started. It was a long climb out of Croyde and the pony was not a fast one. We took it in turns to ride in the jingle and so were saved the fatigue of long unending tramping. Blackberries were everywhere and red admiral butterflies fluttered about in crowds.

Once away from the sea and sheltered from the winds in the high-banked Devon lanes it was very hot and sultry, thunder was in the air. 'Golly! isn't it hot?' panted Ethel, after a particularly stiff bit of climbing. 'I wish I hadn't to wear clothes. They get so sticky,' and she wriggled about. 'Auntie, mayn't I take some of them off? There's no one about.'

'You haven't got much to take off, I should think,' laughed Muriel, 'no stockings and not much else as far as I can see.'

'I've got a chemise, knickers, blouse, and skirt. It's the knickers that stick so, they're so tight. Mayn't I take them off?'

'Have you forgotten the first afternoon?'

'Oh, that was different, we didn't know each other so well then. But now we've no secrets from each other, have we, Auntie darling?' She ran to Muriel and put her arms round her.

'Did you ever know such a creature?' smiled Muriel. 'If you do, remember you leave yourself quite unprotected, and there are lots of nice switches in these hedges.'

'I'll risk that,' shouted Ethel in high glee, as she raised her skirt without any attempt at concealment and undid the buttons of her knickers. She pulled them down and stepped out of them. 'That's better,' she shouted as she threw them into the jingle. 'You stay there! Oh, Auntie, it is lovely to have no drawers on, there's such a lovely draught blowing up my legs.'

'Ethel, for shame,' said Gladys.

'Shocked again, Miss Modesty!' laughed Ethel, running up to her sister. 'Poor thing, she wouldn't be without *her* drawers for the world, would she?' And she danced round her, snatching at her sister's skirt and pretending to pull it up.

'Cecil, cut me that switch,' said Muriel. 'Come here,' she called.

'Oh no, Auntie, it's not fair, I didn't mean anything . . . ' But Muriel had caught her, deftly turned her over and raised her skirt, and gave her naked bottom four smart cuts. Then she let her go. The blows were not really hard, given more to act as a warning and to show her power.

'I told you, you would be quite unprotected,' she laughed.

'Lucky it's a quiet lane,' I said.

'It would have been all the more fun if it hadn't been,' whispered Muriel back to me.

We reached a meadow on top of the hill, through which there was a right of way. It was bounded on one side by the railway line, and had at one time, I should fancy, formed part of a park, for several fine old oaks were still standing. Under one of these we spread the lunch, and sprawled about at our ease. A wood to our west kept the wind away and the sun poured down upon us. Lunch finished, cigarettes whiled away the time, until at last 'an exposition for sleep' came upon me, as it did to Bottom. I slept in perfect content for some time, flat on my back, enjoying a delightfully amorous dream, but was wakened at last by what I thought was a fly tickling my face. I brushed it away several times, but it always returned, and at last in despair I opened my eyes and found that little minx Ethel was tickling me with a blade of grass. Gladys and Juliette were watching the fun and laughing – Muriel was asleep. I sprang up quickly to go for Ethel, seizing the willow switch which I had kept by me. To my surprise when I got to my feet I found my trousers slipping down round my legs. Shrieks of laughter came from all three girls. I hastily pulled the trousers up, intending to enquire about them later, and gave chase to Ethel. The young devil could run like a hare, and I had to put my best leg forward to catch her. In my efforts it was not only my best leg that was forward, for I had only done up the top button of my trousers in my hurry, and John Thomas, ever eager to be in the midst of things, worked his way out. It must have been an edifying spectacle.

At last Ethel tripped on a tussock of grass and came down. Like a flash I was on her and had her clothes up in a twinkling. She squealed for mercy, half-laughing and out of breath. 'You little devil,' I said as I spanked her, 'I'll teach you to wake me up; I'll tickle you; how do you like that, eh?'

'Oh, Uncle, don't, don't.'

'And how dare you undo my trousers?'

'It wasn't me, it wasn't truly, only your thing was sticking up so much that I noticed it, and pointed it out to Gladys and Juliette, and she said it was a shame to keep it tied up close like that, you must be dreaming, and if we waited we should see something funny happen, so she undid your trousers . . . oh don't, Uncle, don't; I didn't touch your trousers, I didn't really. Whip Juliette, she did it, not me, oh my poor bottom, you *do* hurt.'

I left her and went back to the other two. Something in my manner must have scared them, for they got up as I approached. I quickened my steps, and without waiting for me to get near, their guilty consciences urged them to flee. I pursued Gladys first and easily caught her.

'Now, young lady,' I said. 'Who undid my trousers?'

'I didn't, Uncle, really. It was Juliette.'

'But you let her do it, and laughed at me when I got up. You are just as bad as she. Come here, where are your drawers?' I put my hand up under her skirt and, pretending that I thought she wore open drawers, felt between her legs for the opening.

'Oh, Uncle, don't, not here.'

I tucked her head under my left arm and turned her skirt up, then quickly unbuttoned the drawers, each side, and pulled down the flap. Her hands came round at once to cover her bottom and pull down the chemise. 'Take those hands away, and lift your chemise . . . higher . . . higher. That's better.'

'Oh, Uncle, not in the open field; anyone might pass, oh don't; whip me when we get home if you like, but not here . . . oh! there's a man!'

I turned to look and, turning, let her go; she was off like a hare for cover. I could not see anybody and went after her. She dodged a bit but couldn't keep it up for long. I caught her again. 'I don't see any man. Where is he?'

'I . . . don't know, I thought I'd get away. There wasn't a man really. Oh, Uncle, let me go now, do please.'

'Oh wasn't there; well, it would have been just the same if there had been. Now, shall I take your drawers down or will you?' She didn't answer, so I put my hand again up her skirt, found the buttons, and this time undid them all. Then I bent her over under my arm, pulled the drawers right down to her ankles, and began. 'I'm going to give you two whippings, first for laughing at me, and second for trying to tell me lies to escape. You might have got off with one. There – there – there.' From the position in which I held her the blows fell obliquely down and not straight across. The little switch curled wickedly around her legs and between her thighs. After one or two cuts, which evidently reached the tenderest spots, she began to beg for mercy. Her legs swung out here and there trying to dodge the cuts, and ever and anon I had a glimpse of the little virginal crack and the soft fair hair just beginning to shield it. When her bottom began to show marks, I let her go, as I did not want to hurt her really. But where was Juliette? She was nowhere to be seen. There was no trace of her in the field. Ethel was sitting quietly on the grass with her skirt spread out round her – 'to cool her scorched sit-upon,' as she said. 'Where's Juliette?' I asked.

'Ah,' she grinned, 'wouldn't you like to know?' I threatened her with the switch. 'Oh no, no! don't . . . She ran in there with Auntie,' pointing to the wood.

I went towards the wood calling to Juliette, but could see no sign of either of them. 'Come out, you two,' I called. 'Muriel, if you try to hide Juliette, it'll be the worse for you.' But no answer came and at last I gave up the chase and returned to the girls.

'Can't you find 'em?' said Ethel.

'Oh, they can wait,' I answered. 'Let's boil the kettle for tea. How's the sit-upon, Ethel? Cooler?'

'Yes, thank you, you big bully!'

'And how's yours, Gladys? Let me see.' I turned towards her, where she was sitting, and rolled her over, pulling up her skirt. She only made a half-hearted effort to resist and I smoothed and fondled all the parts which I had made to tingle a little time before. She snuggled close to me.

'You *are* cruel to me, Uncle, but I love you so.' I kissed her sweet lips, and John Thomas urged me to throw all scruples aside.

'Here, that's not fair; if you make a fuss of Gladys, you must make a fuss of me too,' said Ethel, and she flung herself on top of me, straddling across my lap. This was too much. I ripped my trousers open and out sprang his Lordship eager for anything. Ethel seized him and, pressing her naked stomach against him, began rubbing furiously. She hadn't long to wait. 'Oh, it's lovely to feel it there,' she cried. 'Oh, what a mess! isn't it hot? . . . But that's where it ought to go, isn't it? Take your hand away.' Before I knew what she was about, she wiped some of the flood from her stomach and rubbed it against her eager slit. 'There, Gladys, there's some for you,' she went on, as she did the same to her sister. 'Auntie shan't have all of him.'

For a moment I was nervous, but realised at once that of course there could be no danger of consequences. The kettle beginning to boil diverted our attention, and at the same time we heard a voice from behind us, 'May we come out, please?'

I assumed a natural tone as if everything was safe for them. 'Oh yes, tea's quite ready, where did you get to?' Muriel and Juliette appeared, the latter quite nervous. 'All right, young woman,' I said, 'you wait till we get home. Why didn't you answer me? Where were you?'

Muriel laughed, 'Well, Cecil, there *are* times and seasons, especially at picnics, when it makes for greater comfort all round for ladies to retire to solitude; you were busy with Gladys, so we seized the opportunity.'

'That's all very well, but Juliette had other reasons for hiding, and you helped her; you won't escape like that, you were harbouring a criminal, as the law puts it, and so share her guilt. You'll pay for it later, both of you. Now tea!'

There wasn't much to put back in the baskets when we had finished. 'Now I suppose we had better start for home,' said Muriel.

'Wait a moment,' I replied, 'Juliette has got to have a whipping first, so have you!'

'Don't be silly, Cecil, it's too late . . . besides, you can't here.'

'Why not? I've whipped the girls, and you whipped Ethel in the lane. Now you can't get away this time and hide. So who's going to be first. I think you had better, for the girls can hold Juliette, and I'm afraid you'd be too strong for them. So come on.'

'I won't; I won't be whipped in a field, before the girls; besides, I haven't done anything . . . Don't be silly, Cecil, or I shall get angry.'

'Angry! What do you mean! How dare you talk to me like that? Go down on your knees at once and pull up your skirts, unless you want me to whip you by force here, and then thrash you when I get home as well. Gladys and Ethel, see that Juliette doesn't get away. Now Muriel, are you going to do as I tell you?' She made no answer or movement, so, to hurry her up, I cut her across her thin skirt with the switch. She closed with me and tried to wrest the switch away from me. We struggled for a moment, but I managed to get her skirt up round her waist, exposing her knickers and chemise – she wore no petticoat. I bent her gradually over and got her head under my arm. At that moment the sound of a train in the distance was heard. 'Cecil,' gasped Muriel, 'there's a train coming, let me get up.'

'It'll be all the more fun,' I whispered, quoting her own words. The train drew nearer. I had dropped the switch in the struggle, intending to use my hand. By this time I had her well tucked away under my arm, with her chemise drawn up and her drawers well opened. Her bottom and sex were fully exposed to view. I deliberately turned her round so that this prospect faced the railway, and spanked her as the train approached. It was an excursion train from Ilfracombe, very long and very full – going slowly up the gradient. There must have been fully two or three hundred people in it, and every window seemed to be full of faces. They evidently spotted us, for above the noise of the train I clearly heard loud cheers; and handkerchiefs seemed to spring out like magic. Of course it was past in a minute, but I cannot adequately describe the fierce joy that I felt in the knowledge that at least two hundred strangers had seen Muriel's bare posterior, growing red under my palm. I saw red for the moment and rained a perfect hail of blows on her devoted cheeks. She sobbed and implored me to let her go. 'I shall die of shame,' she kept on saying. At last I thought I had given her enough and let her go. She crept away without a word, not looking at any of us, and flung herself down under the tree, her whole body heaving with choking sobs. I let her have her cry out and turned to Juliette. The incident of the train had left them all speechless. 'Now, Juliette,' I said. She got up without a word and tottered towards me. 'Are you going to resist or . . . ?'

'Oh, get it over quickly, for God's sake.' She could barely frame the words, she was so nervous.

'Pull your skirts up then and kneel down.' She made no complaint or any sound but meekly did as she was told. I took the switch and, pulling her drawers apart, gave her a swift sound whipping. Her bottom and thighs flinched at the strokes, but she uttered no cry. Only when I had finished I saw that she was crying silently.

I went to Muriel. She was still lying where she had flung herself down. I touched her on the shoulder. She shivered under my touch.

'Go away, leave me . . . I can never look anyone in the face again . . . How do I know who might have been in that train?'

'Don't be silly. They only saw your bottom. They can't recognise you by that!'

'But the girls! They saw . . . oh . . . oh . . . the shame.' I signed to Gladys and Ethel, and whispered to them to comfort their aunt. 'Make a fuss of her,' I said meaningly to Gladys, and turned to help Juliette load the jingle. I heard whispers between the others and kisses, and at last out of the corner of my eye I saw Ethel's hand disappear under her aunt's skirt, while Gladys, kneeling down, put her arms round Muriel's neck. The events of the afternoon had excited me extremely, and though I had had one moment of relief, John Thomas was quite anxious again to play a leading part in the drama. I led Juliette round to the other side of the jingle and, without wasting any time in prelimi-naries, gave him all he wanted.

'I score after all,' said Juliette, wiping her lips, 'but you're a bad boy. Cecil, you must make it up to Muriel!'

'It's good for her; it'll prevent her getting out of hand. I bet the girls have calmed her down.'

We found them in a tangled heap of legs and arms when we went to them. They got up, and though Muriel was decidedly ill at ease for part of the way home, she managed to whisper to me, as we came near the lights of the village, 'It was too bad of you, Cecil.'

'But *you* were quite right,' I answered. 'It *was* much more fun.'

❧ 8 ❧

Foul Weather

The sou'-wester and clear Lundy were no false prophets. The weather broke in the night, and I woke to find the rain lashing the sand. Everywhere was a grey haze. The roar of the breakers was incessant and almost terrifying. Five long ridges of white foam were always to be seen, the farthest being quite far out to sea, while beyond them the sea was a grey tumbling mass, flecked everywhere with white-horses.

Lundy was invisible. At times when the sea-fog drifted it was even impossible to see Baggy Point.

Bathing was out of the question. Even to go out of doors at all required some determination. Now and again some of us ventured during a lull in the rain to brave the elements, but it was only to return quite soon, drenched to the skin and ready to change into dry clothes and get warm by the fire, which fortunately burnt brightly in the kitchen.

The cottage was not adapted for a large party in wet weather. Games of all kinds were tried, and tired of, and tempers were tried too. Hide-and-seek all over the house proved the most popular, and lasted for quite a long time, ending only when Juliette after a long and fruitless search discovered Muriel and Gladys hiding together in rather compromising circumstances. Since the episode of the passing train Muriel had seemed to make a dead set at Gladys; whether she was taking this way of avenging herself on me, or whether she realised that Gladys – alone perhaps of all of us – would understand her deep shame at the indecent exposure, I don't know. But whatever the reason, she certainly singled her out for most pressing attentions.

When Juliette spied them unmistakably in each other's arms, under a bed, she didn't cry out her discovery but went and fetched me quietly. 'What do you think of that?' she asked.

'Disgraceful!' I said, assuming a most virtuous air (I had been similarly employed with Ethel but had not been discovered, so I could preach). 'I am shocked and surprised. We cannot, it seems, play even the most innocent games but they are made the opportunity for impropriety and licence. This must be stopped and punished. Muriel and Gladys, get up at once. Gladys, do your drawers up; I am disgusted with you. Juliette, bring me a cane.'

Muriel stood up. 'Don't be silly, Cecil; you know you wish you had been here, it's only because you weren't in on the scene that you talk like that. It's simply because you want things badly, as I can see, that you're annoyed with us for enjoying ourselves.

'Impertinence won't do you any good, and rude remarks about my physical energy will have to be paid for. Thank you, Juliette,' as she brought the cane. 'Now you two, to begin with, you shall both apologise on your knees to that part of me to which you, Muriel, have so rudely referred, and then kiss it in token of adoration, and then you shall receive a fair punishment for your secret lubricity. Come, Gladys, on your knees; Juliette, fetch Ethel so that she may profit by the lesson.'

Gladys knelt down humbly, looking lovingly up at me. I undid my trousers and let John Thomas have the freedom he wanted. Certainly Muriel had not overstated his case, he looked ready for anything. 'Now kiss him.' Gladys obeyed and I felt her soft lips tenderly caressing the sensitive tip. The effect of her touch was electric. Big as he was before, John Thomas seemed to swell and stiffen visibly; I did not dare allow her to continue, but turned to Muriel. 'Now, Muriel, it's your turn.'

'I won't, I don't want to kiss the beastly thing, take it away,' and she slapped it smartly. I seized her by the shoulders and forced her to her knees.

'Now kiss it, or it will be the worse for you.'

'I won't, I won't, I . . . ' But I pushed it violently against her face and began to rub it over her cheeks. The previous excitement and Gladys's tongue had well prepared the way, and almost at once Muriel's face was spattered with the thick white jets. Some even lodged in her hair. She opened her mouth to speak, but before she could say a word, I thrust him between her lips, just in time for her to receive the extreme libation.

'Now,' I said, 'we must get to business. Lie across the bed, both of you; Juliette, hold them down if necessary; Ethel, I don't think you should look at your aunt's nakedness, so you had better face me – so, yes, kneel down. One moment though, take your sister's drawers down, and turn your aunt's skirt up and pull her drawers apart. I think as they were naughty together, they should be punished together, so we'll tie their legs to each other.' I took a stocking of Muriel's which was handy and tied her left ankle to Gladys's right, and then placed them on the bed as far apart from each other as I could. This naturally opened their legs somewhat and revealed their most intimate retreats – the one not quite fully developed, with lips of pale coral and a light covering of young fair hair, the other perfectly formed, shaded with brown curls and revealing bright red lips, just parted as if asking for a kiss. 'Now Ethel, don't look like that at your auntie, I told you not to.'

'Oh, Uncle, but isn't Auntie's pussy lovely,' she whispered. 'I should love to kiss it.'

'Well, you may kiss it just once, to show her that I am not hard-hearted, and you can kiss Gladys's too, but then you must turn your head and kiss me.' Gladys had made no attempt to resist, and Juliette's hand on her back had shown Muriel that resistance was useless. They had not heard Ethel's whispered request to me, nor my reply, so that the touch of soft lips between her thighs came as a complete surprise. She gave a little gasp and exclamation, and then stretched her legs as wide apart as she could. I did not intend, however, that Ethel should give her the supreme pleasure, so I drew her away and pointed to Gladys. The latter evidently had not realised that she was so exposed, for the cry she gave was more of nervousness than of pleasure and she put one hand behind her, trying to cover her nakedness, and drew her legs together.

'That's enough, Ethel, now turn round.' She obeyed and fastened her lips on my still-eager engine. 'After the oysters comes the bill. Now you must pay for your pleasure.' And I brought the cane smartly down on each bottom, one after the other. From where I stood I could reach both easily. I played with them at first, not striking in any order. Now I would give them alternate cuts of equal strength; now Muriel would receive a couple of stingers with a light featherlike caress in between. Then I would play with Gladys, giving her, say, half a dozen dainty little flicks in and out between her cheeks, and then a couple that drew cries from her and left their mark.

All this time Ethel was busy kissing and sucking, holding me close to her with one hand and with the other exploring all that she could reach through my open trousers. As I felt the consummation approaching, my cuts became more random. Sighs and cries came from both my victims, until at last I saw Gladys's hand reach out and find and clutch Muriel's, as if for sympathy. The latter's thighs began to contract and heave, but Gladys evidently felt no such approach of pleasure. I knelt behind her and just managed to reach her dainty lips with my tongue, while I still continued to spur on Muriel with the cane. Ethel did not let go of me but crouched lower and lower. At last the supreme moment came for all three of us, practically simultaneously, and as I gave Ethel all my manhood, I drank down Gladys's sweet life, while my eyes feasted on Muriel's reddened cheeks and glistening lips, from which trickled great pearly drops of passion.

This little orgy calmed us for some hours. After dinner we all felt tired, and Muriel said at once she was going to lie down and sleep. I said I would follow her example. So she and Juliette retired to her room, and I went to mine. I had not been there long and was just dozing when a tap came at the door, and I heard Ethel's voice, 'May we come in and lie down beside you, Uncle? We'll be quite quiet, but it's dull being alone.'

'All right,' I said.

'Come along, Gladys,' said Ethel, and the two girls came in.

I had undressed and put on my pyjamas for comfort. When Ethel saw this, she said, 'Oh, let's undress too,' and she slipped off her skirt and blouse and quickly got out of her knickers. 'Oh go on, Gladys, don't be shy.' Gladys blushed divinely, but the temptation was too great and she slowly and discreetly undressed to her chemise. She was very modest and careful, however, and though I watched her every movement, she let me see no higher than halfway up her thigh.

Ethel was already in bed snuggling close up to me when Gladys crept in. 'Isn't this lovely!' said Ethel as she pulled up her chemise and twined her legs round one of mine. Her mischievous hand sought between my legs as she looked up at me with a roguish smile.

'No, you mustn't do that. We mustn't tire ourselves out,' I said, pushing her hand away.

'It's all very well for you and Gladys,' she answered, 'you've both had your fun this morning, even though Gladys did get a whipping as well. I've had nothing. I'd willingly have had a whipping, if I could have had the other things as well.'

'Poor precious girl, were you left out in the cold? It's a shame. We must see what we can do.' So I found her delicious little slit with my left hand and began to play with it, while my right hand caressed Gladys's young breasts.

'Ah, that's lovely, get your finger right in, oh what are you doing?' I was letting my hand wander slightly and while one finger was penetrating the virgin lips, the other was exploring another adjacent retreat. She wriggled and twisted under the double pleasure. Her eyes dilated, her mouth opened as the quick gaspy sighs came ever faster; she thrust her body down on my fingers, and at last flinging her arms round my neck, she fastened her lips on my shoulder and I felt her sharp teeth nipping my flesh. Then she collapsed limply and her eyes closed. In five minutes she was asleep.

Gladys's regular breathing on the other side of me showed that she had not waited for her sister to set her the example. Her bosom rose and fell under my hand; it would have been a shame to disturb either of them, so I let them sleep on.

❦ 9 ❧

An 'Evening Continuation Class'

Next day the weather improved somewhat; we were able to get out, though the sea was still too rough for bathing. The rain came on again, however, during the afternoon, and we were prisoners again for the evening.

After tea Muriel said, 'What shall we do? Cards? Hide-and-seek? Or what? I'm ready for anything.'

'Hide-and-seek again! Are you eager for a repetition of yesterday, you two? . . . No, I tell you what, let's play school!'

'Oh yes,' said Muriel mischievously, 'I'll be mistress.' Ethel made a wry face and rubbed her little sit-upon meaningly.

'That wouldn't be much of a change, would it, Ethel?' I laughed. 'No, let's be fair. Let's draw lots for mistress, and she can choose her own monitor to help to keep order, and the rest of us must promise to submit and play fair.' Muriel looked doubtful. 'Come,' I urged, for I knew what she was thinking. 'It will be all the more fun if one of the girls draws the lot.'

'Ooh, I hope I do,' shouted Ethel; 'look out for yourself if I do, Uncle Cecil.'

'Oh, very well then, just for this once, it's only a game. But I don't understand about the monitor. What's her position? Can she punish; and can she be punished, just like the others?'

I thought a moment. 'That depends on the mistress. If she likes to hand over powers she can. Of course, the monitor must submit to discipline too.'

'I see,' she answered. 'Come along then, let's draw lots.'

I cut up five pieces of paper, and on one of them I drew a birch, as symbol of office, folded them up and shook them in a hat.

'Now then, who'll draw first?'

'Me please,' said Ethel quickly – she was dancing with excitement. 'Oh, blank . . . no luck!'

Juliette and Gladys both drew blanks. Then remained myself and

Muriel. 'Oh lor, we're in for it,' whispered Ethel to the others.

'You're the first,' said Muriel to me. I chose one of the papers – it was a blank. 'I've got it then,' shouted Muriel in high glee. 'Look out for yourselves.'

'Choose your monitor,' I said, 'you're mistress for half an hour.'

'Not very long.'

'Quite long enough for a game. Come, who will you have for monitor?'

'I'll have . . . ' She looked quickly at each of us. 'I'll have Gladys . . . Gladys, go to my room and get the cases, I'm sure we shall want them and it will save time later. Now you children sit over there and behave yourselves or . . . ! Cecil, don't wriggle about. Juliette, sit up straight.'

Ethel was giggling with suppressed excitement; I entered into the spirit of the game and, playing the schoolboy as well as I could, I began pinching Juliette's bottom secretly. She stood it for some time, for she did not want to start the ball rolling, but at last Muriel noticed her wriggling about. 'Juliette,' she called, 'stand up; what are you wriggling about for?'

'Cecil was pinching me.'

'Is that true, Cecil? Where was he pinching you?'

'On the bottom.'

'How dare you use such words. Hold out your hand . . . now the other; go back to your place. Cecil, come here. How dare you behave like that and pinch Juliette on a place which I will not name.' She assumed the schoolma'am manner admirably. 'It is only right that you should suffer in the same place. Take your trousers down.'

'Oh please let me off this time,' I began to whimper, 'I won't do it again.'

'Certainly not, take your trousers down at once.'

'I won't.'

'Oh very well; Gladys, take them down for him.' Gladys hesitated. 'Will you obey me, Miss, or shall I have to punish you as well?' She made the cane whistle in the air just behind Gladys's back. Gladys came towards me and began to untie the sash I wore round my waist. Then she began to undo the buttons. 'Don't take too long over it, or I shall be suspicious of what you're doing.' Gladys blushed very red and quickly undid the rest. 'Now pull them down.' The trousers fell round my knees. 'Now bend him over the couch and lift his shirt-tail. Go down lower, Cecil; lower still. Lower . . . lower . . . there!' Certainly Muriel meant to play the scene for all it was worth. The cane fell with all her strength right across both cheeks. 'You naughty boy, I'll teach you to pinch your schoolfellows. Will you be good in future? Will you? Will you?' She gave me six cuts in all, and I was not sorry when she stopped. 'Now go and stand in the corner with your face to the wall. Keep your shirt up so that your punishment may act as a warning to the others.' The humiliation of my position was acute, and I was half-inclined to regret having started the game; but I determined to play the sporting game and wait my time for a chance of getting my own back. The knowledge too that Gladys and Ethel were looking at my nakedness was quite exciting, and I felt my passion rising within me.

The spectacle evidently pleased the others as well, for I heard a giggle from Ethel, and Muriel's voice, 'What are you laughing at?'

'He looks so funny, oh, isn't he marked!'

'There's nothing to laugh at, young lady, as you'll soon find out. Gladys, take Ethel and smack her soundly for me. I am tired.'

'I won't be smacked by Gladys.'

'Oh won't you! You will do as your schoolmistress tells you.'

Ethel realised it was no good to resist, and perhaps thought it would be wiser to submit to her sister than to risk the heavier hand of Muriel. 'Lay her across your knee, Gladys, undo her drawers, now take this brush and spank her naughty little bottom; we will see if she will think other people's punishments are so funny in the future. Harder than that, harder, I say, harder! I shall have to show you myself how to do it if you won't obey me.'

I could hear the note of gloating pleasure in Muriel's voice. Gladys did not seem to put much heart into her blows. Muriel began to lose patience or at any rate pretended to. 'If you don't whip her properly I shall whip you, monitress though you are. Stand up, lay Ethel across the couch. Now smack her as I tell you.'

'Hasn't she had enough?'

'Enough? Why, you haven't made her turn even pink. Will you do as you're told? Take that then!' I heard the cane fall across Gladys's skirt, and immediately a harder, crisper smack from the brush on Ethel's naked skin. 'That's better, I see you want an example. There you are then, again, again, again!'

Ethel began to squeal just a little, Muriel's object-lesson was evidently proving effective. I looked at my watch. 'Time's up,' I said, as I stooped to pick up my trousers.

'Hooray!' said Ethel, turning round and rubbing herself. 'You just wait, my girl,' she went on to her sister, 'if I draw the lucky paper won't I tan you!'

'Only four lots this time,' I said, 'no one can be mistress twice.' I folded up the papers again, but this time I kept the lucky one in my hand and when Ethel was about to draw slipped it into her hand without the others seeing. She just gave me a quick look but otherwise made no sign, and proceeded to pretend to choose deliberately. When she opened it her joy was unbounded. 'I've got it, I've got it, oh what fun. Uncle Cecil, you be my monitor and tell me what to do!'

'Well,' I said, 'I'm sure they're all very naughty and deserve a whipping. I should whip them all round first, it will make a good beginning.'

'Good idea. I'll begin with Gladys, before my own bottom stops smarting. Come on, Miss, come and lie across my knee, at once. Pull your skirt up, open those knickers and keep them open – wide open unless you want your knuckles cracked.'

It was absolutely lovely to see the flushed eager face, the eyes sparkling with naughtiness as Ethel prepared to chastise her sister's soft pink bottom. 'I'll show you how to whip. There, there, there.' The brush fell quickly here, there and everywhere, all over the plump surface. 'I don't want anyone to show me how to do it. Do I, Uncle?'

Muriel whispered to me, 'I say, Cecil, I don't know that I quite like this.'

'Nervous?'

'Well . . . '

'Mind, if she wants to whip *you*, you'll have to submit.'

'I don't think . . . '

'If you *don't*,' I said quite seriously, 'I'll flog you till you can't stand, in front of her. You consented to play the game, and must go on with it.' She saw that I meant what I said, and said no more, though she turned a little pale.

Gladys's whipping was still going on, her bottom was a rosy pink. 'There, that will do for the present, for you,' said Ethel. 'Now will you whip Juliette, Uncle, please. She's not been very naughty, but I think a little whipping will do her good.'

'Come on, Juliette,' I said, 'I'm not to do it too hard, it seems; so I'll use a birch. Take your drawers off and get on the couch.' Ethel watched all the preparations with eager eyes. When Juliette, in slipping her drawers down, showed all herself both back and front, Ethel whispered to me: 'Hasn't she got a lot of whiskers?'

'Ssh!' I said, and raised the birch. I gave her about a dozen moderate cuts, hard enough to be felt and to leave just a few faint marks. 'Is that enough?'

'Make it curl in there, in between,' pointing to where we could just see the pouting lips of her sex. I did as she told me. Juliette began to wriggle. She was always most sensitive to the birch. 'She seems to like that,' said Ethel, 'give her some more.' I went on until I saw by the nervous contraction of the thighs and the opening and shutting of the lips that the final paroxysm was approaching, and at last was rewarded by the sight of a few pearly drops appearing.

Ethel looked on wide-eyed. 'What's happened? Have you made her come?' she whispered. I nodded. She ran to Juliette and inserted two of her fingers. Juliette gave a gasp and imprisoned the intrusive hand between her thighs. 'Oh, you naughty girl,' said Ethel, 'you deserve another whipping for that.'

'I think she's had enough,' I said, 'and there's still Muriel,' I whispered.

Ethel looked at me and then at Muriel. 'I don't like to . . . '

'Don't you want to?'

'*Don't I!* But . . . '

'Frightened?'

'Um!' she nodded.

'Oh, she won't mind, it's only a game. You see . . . Muriel,' I said, raising my voice, 'Ethel is frightened to whip you. I tell her you won't mind, as it's only a game.' I said this very meaningly, looking her straight between the eyes.

She laughed nervously, and then said, trying to speak naturally: 'Of course, dear, fair's fair; how would you like to do it?' And she stood up.

'Shall I horse her?'

'What's that?'

'I take her pick-a-back. Then you can whip both of us at the same time.' I undid my trousers as I said this and let them fall. 'Now Muriel, get ready, off with your drawers, and I'll pin your skirt up. Now get up on that chair.'

'But, Cecil, she'll see everything.'

'So much the better, she'll like that, come on.' I tucked her legs well under my arms, she put her arms round my neck, and we stood waiting.

'What shall I use?' said Ethel.

'Anything you like; you'll find a birch the best.'

'I don't quite like to . . . '

'Don't be a silly girl,' said Muriel. 'Make haste. I've told you, you may; don't keep me exposed like this.'

'Don't you mind her, Ethel,' I said. 'You keep her exposed as long as you like; is she properly exposed, can you see everything?'

'Yes,' whispered the girl, in a shamed whisper.

'Well, go on then, whip her, whip all you can see, whip me too.' My imagination had fired me. I wanted to hear the cuts fall on Muriel's flesh and to know that her most secret parts were exposed to the greedy gaze of 'the mistress' and were quivering under her blows. Strangely enough I wanted also to feel the blows myself. A strange mixture of sadism and masochism filled me, my emotion was almost too much for me; my throat seemed choked; I could barely breathe; and it was a positive relief to me when I heard the first blow – a very light one – fall on Muriel's plump flesh, and then felt a light caress from the rod on my own skin.

Emboldened by taking the first step, Ethel's blows became heavier and quicker. As she went on, she left me more alone and concentrated more of her attention on Muriel. At last the lust of flogging got the better of her and I heard the blows fall quicker and quicker. They were evidently more effective too, for Muriel began to twist about on my shoulders. I had hard work to keep her legs under my arms. At last, 'That's enough,' she said, and Ethel stopped at once. 'Let me down, Cecil,' she said to me.

I was by no means satisfied. My whole nature was burning with ungratified desire. I must find relief somehow. 'I don't think you've had by any means enough, and I know I haven't. I'll finish you off if Ethel doesn't, I know you're not satisfied either, are you? Come here, let me see,' and I put my hand between her legs and drew her to me. 'No, I thought not; bend over that table; Juliette, come and kneel here before me, and you two girls whip me, both of you. Go on, do as I tell you or I'll whip you. I tell you I want you to whip me, I want it.'

I think I must have been almost mad with unsatisfied passion. Probably the 'strenuous' life I had been leading and the exciting scenes I had just witnessed were responsible for my condition, but I felt I must experience every possible sensation at once. I seized a birch and began to flog Muriel lasciviously. Juliette was kneeling before me kissing me, and the two girls were nervously attacking me behind. They were too nervous to satisfy me, however. 'Harder, harder,' I said to them, but it was no good. At last I told Juliette to change places with Gladys. The effect was instantaneous. Juliette knew her business thoroughly. She was a past-mistress in her art. Her clever manipulation with the rod, coupled with Gladys's clinging lips and tongue, acted like a charm. I felt the thrills begin to run through my body, and just as Muriel's bottom began to heave quicker and quicker and to twist every way under the prying twigs, I yielded with one supreme effort and gave Gladys what seemed to be my *very soul*.

❧ 10 ❧

A Morning's Adventure

It was perhaps fortunate that the storm cleared away in the night, for a succession of wet days and the consequent indoor amusements might have proved rather enervating for all of us. As it happened, however, the next day broke fine and bright, and we were all able to get our early morning bathe in brilliant sunshine. The night-school had taken away any few remnants of reserve on the part of Muriel before the girls, and all five of us met on an absolutely level footing. Ethel boldly appeared absolutely naked, and skipped about careless of anyone. Muriel attempted a protest, but I would hear nothing of that kind, and when she began to argue that all discipline would vanish if the young madam was allowed to go on like that, I told her straight that after being whipped on her naked bottom by Ethel, she could not take up any attitude of superiority. 'Any discipline necessary, *I* will exercise – and on all of you. So don't presume.' She looked mutinous. 'Do you dare to question my authority?'

'No, Cecil, but ... '

'But what? . . . You'll do exactly as I tell you, do you hear? *Exactly!* And to prove it, take that bathing dress off at once. Take it off!' We were just at the edge of the sea, the others were dancing about in the surf, Ethel's white body gleaming through the waves. 'Take it off now – undo those buttons.' As she hesitated, I brought my hand heavily down across her wet flank. The noise of the smack attracted the attention of the others. Muriel uttered a little cry in protest. '*Will* you do as I tell you? Take that costume off at once or . . . ' I seized a long trail of seaweed which had been washed up by the tide and made it curl round her legs.

'Oh, don't, Cecil, don't!'

'Well, do as I tell you.'

'But I can't take it off here.'

'Why not?' I went to her and seized the costume by the neck and with a quick jerk ripped it right open down the front, tearing all the buttons off. It fell apart showing her breasts and body down below the navel. 'Now, get out of it quickly,' and I plied the seaweed actively all over her. She saw that it was no good resisting and as rapidly as she could disengaged herself from the clinging garment.

'Oh, look at Auntie!' shouted Ethel. 'She's taking her dress off. Come on, Gladys, take yours off too. It's much nicer being naked in the sea.' She ran up to her sister and began to unbutton her dress, Gladys resisted, but she could not prevent Ethel's quick fingers. The costume fell apart and her beautiful budding breasts and fair body appeared.

'That's right!' I shouted, as, with stinging cuts of the wet seaweed, I helped Muriel to hurry over getting out of the legs of her costume. 'Now Juliette, take yours off too.'

'I won't,' said Juliette.

'Oh won't you!' and I turned towards her. She fled at my approach, running up the sand towards the cottage. I followed her, but she could run very fast and had she not slipped and stumbled I doubt whether I could have caught her. As it was, I came up to her as she lay panting and rained a shower of blows all over her back and legs. She cried and writhed and at last got to her feet.

'Oh, Cecil, don't! oh that seaweed does hurt! oh! ah!' She skipped and jumped about trying to dodge the blows.

'Take that thing off then! Who are you to object to being as naked as the others? Now, get back to the sea.'

I drove her naked down the beach, touching her up every now and then with the seaweed, and then followed a most enjoyable bathe as I chased each of the four naked girls in turn among the breakers, until at last we all went back to the cottage and dressed for breakfast.

After breakfast we all went out on the beach intending to bathe again before dinner, but, as will be seen, things happened which prevented us.

Muriel suggested that we should go to the left this time and explore further west, so we accordingly struck out. Round the rocks into the west bay we clambered, carrying towels, and while I lay down to bask in the sun, the girls roamed here and there. I noticed a couple of women searching for shellfish and some common children playing about who evidently belonged to them, but I didn't pay much attention to them.

Suddenly I was roused from the half-doze into which I had fallen by cries of anger and squeals of pain. 'I'll teach you to throw sand at me, you little beasts, take that, and that.' And the sound of a palm falling heavily on bare flesh came to my ears. 'Muriel smacking the girls,' I thought, and sat up to watch. The others were at the other end of the beach and I only saw a small group where a struggle was going on. Then to my surprise I saw two small figures break away and run towards the women who were fishing. There was a short colloquy – evidently complaints from the children – and then the two women went quickly towards Muriel, brandishing the short sticks which they used for knocking the shellfish off the rocks. I thought I had better go and see what was happening, so I got up and strolled towards the others. I arrived just after the women reached the group and were beginning to demand satisfaction. 'You smack my Sally, will 'ee?' shouted one. 'I'll pay 'ee,' and she flourished the stick menacingly at Muriel.

'Here, none of that,' I said. 'What's the matter?'

'Her smacked my Sally, and I be 'gwine to pay 'er vor it.'

'Not like that though,' I answered. 'Smack her if you like, but not with the stick; she didn't use the stick. I'll see fair play.' I took the sticks from her and the other woman. 'Now, smack her bottom if you can, I'm sure she deserves it.'

'Cecil,' said Muriel, half-frightened, 'you surely don't mean . . . ' But before she could finish one woman had seized hold of her and the other went for Juliette.

'You girls run away home, we'll come presently; it's no place for you.' Gladys was looking very scared and seemed glad to obey, but Ethel, her whole face alight with eager mischievous curiosity, lingered. 'Go on,' I said, 'or I'll tan that bottom of yours so that you won't know yourself.' The four women had now joined in set battle. Muriel's opponent was a short thickset woman, evidently strong but rather fat; her superior strength was counterbalanced by her lack of agility. Juliette was pitted against a younger and more formidable opponent. She evidently had but a slight chance, and though she wriggled and twisted, I saw that the contest could have but one end. Between Muriel and her antagonist, however, the contest promised to be more level and exciting. The woman tried hard to bend Muriel down under her arm, but the latter wriggled like an eel in her grasp and gripped her quite scientifically. At last I heard the sound of tearing cloth, and half the woman's skirt fell away from the waist, showing a none too clean flannelette smock. 'Tear my skirt, will 'ee?' she shouted, and she redoubled her efforts in retaliation. Rip! Tear! I saw Muriel's light frock come off in ribbons, entangling her legs. A vigorous pull burst the buttons off her satin knickers, they fell round her knees. Hampered like this she was badly handicapped and in a moment she was held tightly under her opponent's left arm and a hurricane of blows from the broad heavy palm fell on the naked cheeks of her bottom.

Juliette by this time had been equally mastered and, from her cries and the sound of smacks, was evidently experiencing a severe treatment. Her bottom was tinged a dull red and her legs were flying every way in her pain. Muriel, though mastered, had not given up the struggle. Her hands were free and seeking for a hold. At last they found the torn skirt, and more of the smock appeared, which in its turn suffered. The merciless palm still descended, however, on her bottom, and her assailant took no notice of the damage done to herself. She simply uttered hoarse pants and growls of rage.

At last Muriel managed to tear off all the clothes she could reach, and laid bare to view the brawny thighs and coarse-skinned bottom. Then, fastening her nails in one cheek, she gripped with all her strength. This evidently made some impression, for the woman twisted away and freed herself. Muriel, however, couldn't escape, for her knickers still hampered her legs. The woman rushed at her again, flung her to the ground face downwards, and began again to belabour her bottom and thighs with both hands.

Muriel began to implore for mercy and I thought it was time to interfere. 'That's enough,' I said. But the woman wouldn't stop. I went towards her and began to pull her off, when I heard the sound of approaching footsteps on the sand. I turned round and saw the two children who had been the cause of all the trouble coming towards us accompanied by four men.

'What be all this about?' said one. I began to tell them shortly, for I didn't like the look of things and wanted to get away. 'You 'old your gab; missus, 'oo tore your dress?' I again tried to explain, but a sudden blow from his hammer-like fist sent me flying, and before I could get up again, I was seized and held down by two of the others. Noisy altercations were going on all this time, and by the time I was able to see what was happening, Muriel and Juliette were in the grasp of two of the men, who were making their wounded bottoms again pay for their chastisement of the children. I struggled to get free but it was no good; I had to lie and watch Muriel and Juliette writhing under the heavy blows of those two savages. The two women stood looking on, enjoying the cruel torture. At last one whispered something to the other. A gleam of fierce joy sprang to the other's eyes. She went up to the man who was belabouring Muriel. I did not catch what she said, but he looked towards me. 'Oh, don't take no notice of 'im. Go on.' To my horror and surprise she undid the man's trousers and let out his rampant engine. I have never seen such a huge horrible affair. I struggled all I knew to escape from the grasp of my captor, but all my efforts were futile. At the same time I must admit an overpowering desire to witness Muriel's supreme humiliation came over me, and I waited and watched with staring eyes and parched throat. With a quick twist the man turned Muriel over and got between her legs before she knew what was happening. When his naked member touched her, however, she gave one terrible shriek and wrenched herself away. She struggled to her feet and tried to run, but the ever-clinging knickers brought her to earth again. The man and the women were on her in a flash. The latter tore away all the impeding skirts and, seizing her legs, held them wide apart while the man got between them and set to work. Shriek after shriek came from Muriel, who flung her body this way and that trying to avoid the thrusting weapon. I heard my name continually in imploring tones, but even if I had been free, I doubt if I could have gone to her assistance. I was absolutely fascinated by the horrible sight of this proud fair body being outraged before my eyes.

At last the man came to the end of his attack. I saw his powerful body heave and plunge, and at last with a grunt more bestial than human he collapsed on Muriel's body, entirely hiding it from view. Then he gathered himself together and stood up, leaving his victim quivering and inert.

'Have 'ee finished, it be my turn now,' said one of my captors. 'Catch hold of this young man.'

He released me as he spoke and the other took his place. I made no resistance. My whole being was one tingle of lascivious excitement. I wanted a whole army of men to throw themselves on Muriel and possess her. The other man approached his victim with gloating eyes. She lay supine, stretched out just as she was from her last sacrifice. When she felt his body close to her she made no movement of resistance. Only a sob came from her lips, and she half-opened her eyes only to close them again as if to avoid the sight of her violator. He was a much younger man than the other, and splendidly built. Also, as Muriel made no resistance, he didn't attack her so brutally. His movements were slower and more gentle. After a moment or two I was surprised to see Muriel open her legs a little, and move her body to meet his thrusts. 'You can leave go 'er legs, missus,' said the man, '' 'er loves me I do believe.' The woman let go as she was told, and Muriel drew up her knees and after a few passionate plunges flung them around the heavy thighs of her lover. Her arms also clutched his woollen jersey, holding him close to her. At last I could see that the final spasm was approaching. Her passion proved too much for the man; before he really was ready for her she drew all his life from him. 'You little bitch,' he shouted, 'I be coming already, I . . . ' He said no more but sought her lips with a fierce kiss. Her lips met his and the two, male and female, forgot all differences of class. The primeval sex instinct overleapt all barriers, and the two natures commingled in elemental passion.

Juliette in the meantime had undergone a similar experience at the hands of her assailant but, realising the hopelessness of resistance, had submitted quietly. The women, seeing that their victims were cowed, watched the scene, but at last the one of them whose skirt was torn said, 'The men be having all the fun, young man, don't 'ee want to enjoy yourself? My man 'ave vucked your missus, wouldn't 'ee like to vuck me?' I made no answer; I certainly did want the pleasure she suggested but not with her. 'Come on,' she said, and made a dive for my trousers where my virility was all too apparent. Luckily, perhaps, my excitement was so great that the touch of her hand gave the finishing touch and before I could stop myself I sprinkled her all over. 'Ah the dirty beast,' she cried, pushing it away. 'Mary, the men be arl used up, come here and do me a kindness.' The other woman came forward and without more ado plunged her hand under the torn skirt, lifting her own at the same time. There was a minute's silent pause and then the two women clutched each other and . . . let go. Muriel and Juliette were free by this time; the men were talking in undertones together. At last the one who seemed to be the leader came to me.

'Now, look 'ere, mister,' he said, 'be you agoin' to make trouble over this mornin's work? 'Cose if you be, you don't leave this beach alive; there's been no real 'arm done. Your missus and this wench 'ave enjoyed it, 'spite of everything, and so 'ave you, you know it. Vair's vair, and if so be you want to vuck our women as we've vucked yours, why there they be. I can't say vairer than that. But if you mean to make trouble, as God's my judge, we'll do vor the lot of 'ee.'

I looked at the two girls, who stood close to each other. There was nothing to be gained by making trouble. The damage, if any, *was* done. I therefore said, 'I think the least said, the soonest mended; these ladies have paid for their fault, rather severely perhaps, but if I promise not to say anything about this morning's work you must swear not to boast of what you've done. And what about these children, who were the cause of the whole trouble?' I pointed to the two girls, who had been spectators of the whole scene.

'Oh, I'll settle them kids, come 'ere Sally and Mary. Be you agoin' to zay a word about this 'ere business?' The two girls shook their heads. 'Well, we'll make zure, come 'ere.' He seized hold of one and, turning her over, belaboured her bottom and thighs with his heavy hand. Then he treated the other the same way. 'That'll larn 'ee, if you ever zo much as breathe a word, I'll tan your 'ides like you've never 'ad it afore, zo you watch it . . . 'ere, missus, you'd better go back to the cottage and clothe yerself. And what about your missus, sir? 'Er can't go 'ome like thiccy.'

'Perhaps your wife could lend her something; here's something for you to buy a new skirt for her.' I slipped a sovereign into his hand.

'You be a proper gentleman,' he said. 'I be sorry if I did wrong in vucking your missus, but if you'd like to vuck mine, why there she is, and I believe her 'ud like it.'

'Oh, that's all right, lend the lady a skirt and we'll get home.'

The women went towards a cottage in the distance. They presented a strange sight as they walked away together. Muriel and Juliette supported each other, scarcely able to stand, the former practically naked from the waist downwards, for her skirt had been torn right off and her chemise was in ribbons. Juliette's clothing had not suffered so much and she presented a slightly more decent figure. In front Muriel's brawny opponent led the way; she too showed, to all who cared to see, her fat red thighs and tattered flannelette smock. She strode ahead like some Amazonian chieftainess proudly bringing her captives home with her. The two children stayed behind with the men near me. The women disappeared into the cottage, and after a minute or two Muriel and Juliette reappeared, the former wearing a coarse skirt, much too big for her, and came towards me. I went to meet them and we silently turned homewards. Neither Muriel nor Juliette said a word as we walked along. They both seemed absolutely broken, and held on to me each to an arm. Every now and then I felt Juliette shudder and sob, but Muriel seemed past all outward display of feeling. I was wondering what Gladys and Ethel thought of the morning's adventure and was afraid lest they should be nervous at our protracted absence. I tried to rouse the two beaten women to some show of self-possession before we met them, and I was just telling them to try to put a good face on it before they met the girls when I spied the corner of a frock disappearing behind a rock. I freed myself and hurried towards it.

I was not altogether surprised to discover Miss Ethel hiding there. 'I thought I told you to go home! What are you doing here? Where's Gladys?'

'She went home. Oh, Uncle, wasn't it awful?'

'So you're been spying, have you? What have you seen?'

'Everything! Oh, Uncle, how horrible! Poor Auntie and Juliette!'

'It'll be *poor Ethel* when we get home. You know what I told you would happen.'

She looked frightened. 'I couldn't help it, Uncle! I *had* to stay and see.'

'Oh did you?' I answered grimly. 'Well, now you'll have to pay for your curiosity. I'll talk to you after dinner. Come along.'

I took her hand and we rejoined the others. 'Ethel has disobeyed me and has been spying,' I said to Muriel. 'We will deal with her after dinner.' Muriel did not seem to take much notice. Her one idea was to get home. When we arrived at the cottage we found Gladys very nervous and frightened.

Oh, I'm so glad you've come, I was getting so anxious. Ethel *would* stay behind; I tried to bring her along but she wouldn't come. I told her you would be angry but she said she didn't care.'

'She'll care, before I've finished with her.'

Ethel made a face. 'Well, if I do get a whipping it was worth it. Come on, Uncle, whip me now and get it over,' she added impudently, lifting up her skirt and exposing her bottom. Probably the beaten aspect of Muriel and Juliette inspired her with courage.

'You go to your room and wait there till I send for you.' As she did not obey, I seized hold of her and dragged her upstairs into her room and locked the door on her. Then I went back to the others. 'Gladys, you can help me; get some hot water.'

I undressed both Muriel and Juliette. Their bottoms and thighs presented a shocking spectacle. They were simply one mass of bruises from thighs right down to the knees. The flesh was all swollen and pulpy, and to my great horror, a small trickle of blood was issuing from Muriel. Her assailant had evidently been too big and too rough for her.

When Gladys returned with the hot water, I laid the two bruised bodies face downwards on the bed, and Gladys and I tenderly sponged the cruelly battered flesh. They could scarcely stand it being touched, low moans greeted every pressure of the sponge. Then I took further precautions. I syringed both of them thoroughly with antiseptic solutions, and after a thorough cleansing I swathed them in oil-soaked bandages and went downstairs to dinner with Gladys.

❧ 11 ❧

The Reward of Spying

We took some food up to Muriel and Juliette, but they were too worn-out to touch it; Gladys asked if Ethel was not going to have any, but I said, 'No; she has been very naughty, and must be punished.'

'I *did* try to get her to come home, Uncle; really I did, but she *would* stop and watch. I knew you would be angry. Oh, Uncle, what happened? It must have been awful, I never saw such bruises, and poor Auntie was bleeding from inside. Did they do other things to her besides whipping her? How could they, they were only women!'

I told her shortly what had happened, and she saw from my fast-colouring eye – the result of my assailant's fist – that I had not altogether escaped.

'How glad I am I came home; if we had been there they might have done it to us! And I don't want anyone else but you, Uncle, to do *that* to me!' She came and sat on my knee and put her arm round my neck, kissing me and murmuring words of love. My hand went immediately under her clothes and unbuttoned her drawers. She made no resistance. Indeed, she moved slightly to allow me to pull them off, and when she was quite free of them she opened her legs wide, inviting my eager caress. I unbuttoned my trousers and placed her willing hand there. She took hold of my rampant affair, and pulling it gently towards her, she whispered, 'Put it there, Uncle, I want it; oh please put it there.'

'No, I mustn't; I promised I wouldn't; not yet.'

'But I want it, I want it.'

'Kiss it instead, and I'll kiss you – lie down on the couch.' She went straight to the couch and lay on her back with open arms and legs, displaying all the perfection of her virgin sex. I bent over her and fastened my lips to the pouting pink slit and began to suck greedily the sweet juice that was already welling up. At the same moment I felt her lips close round my member and the caressing tongue drawing me right into her mouth. She had not long to wait. 'Look out,' I panted, 'it'll happen.'

'I want it,' she answered, 'I want every bit of it.' As I felt the supreme moment approaching, I raised myself slightly and, looking down, could just see her eager lips working round my weapon as it throbbed in ecstasy. She gulped in answer until the flood came too quick for her and she had to draw back, allowing the liquor to spurt all over her face and neck.

I disengaged myself and turned towards her. She smiled up at me. 'It's not very nice, but it's *you*, I love it . . . oh, there's another drop, let me have that.' She drew me towards her and drained the last remaining drops eagerly.

'Now for Miss Ethel,' I said. 'You go up and wash and tell her I'm ready.'

'You won't be too severe with her, will you, Uncle?'

'She must be taught to obey,' I answered, and followed her upstairs.

We found Ethel sitting on the bed, evidently half-frightened, half-defiant. 'I was wondering when you were coming,' she said. 'Isn't dinner ready?'

'*I'm* ready,' I answered. 'Dinner may come later, when you've been punished for your disobedience. Take your things off and come with me.'

'I want my dinner.'

'Do as I tell you, you'll have no dinner yet.'

'I shan't, I want my dinner.'

Gladys was washing her face. 'You'd better do as you're told, Ethel, she said. 'I told you Uncle Cecil would be angry. Don't make it worse for yourself, take your things off, and perhaps he won't be too severe with you.'

'You mind your own business,' retorted Ethel. 'I want my dinner and I mean to have it.'

She made a dart for the door, but I seized her and dragged her struggling to Muriel's room. She fought and kicked and struggled but could not escape.

Once inside the room, I said to Muriel, 'Here is Ethel, who disobeyed me and watched all that took place this morning. Will you punish her, or shall I?'

'You begin, Cecil; I'm too worn-out. Whip her well so that I can see it. Perhaps I'll help later.'

'Now Ethel,' I said, 'are you going to take your things off yourself or shall I have to do it for you? I warn you for your own sake that you had better do it yourself.'

'I want my dinner,' repeated Ethel. I went to the cases, which were in the room, opened one and took out a cane, and brought it smartly across her shoulders. 'Will you obey me?' She uttered a cry as the cane fell across the thin frock, but made no attempt to undress.

Again and again the cane fell. 'Oh please, Uncle, yes, I'll take my things off, I will really.'

'Make haste then,' rapping her across the knuckles as she fumbled with the buttons.

Hot and angry tears appeared in her eyes as she tried to avoid the blows and the dress fell to the ground. The corsets followed, leaving only the chemise covering her slim young body. She began to unfasten that, but I stopped her. 'Keep that on for the present. Now I'm going to whip you severely for your gross disobedience and curiosity. I distinctly told you to go home this morning but you wilfully disobeyed me out of insolent curiosity; in consequence you were witness of your Aunt's and Juliette's shame. Your body will now pay for your disobedience and I will try to make you remember to obey me in the future. Bend forward a little and draw that chemise tight across your back.'

She gave me a frightened look but did as I told her. She evidently expected that her bottom was to suffer, for she drew the chemise tight round her hips, bending forward so that the outline of the cheeks and thighs was clearly revealed. My intentions, however, were different, and I surprised her by directing my cuts across her back. She gave a surprised cry as the cane fell just below her shoulders. The chemise, only half-tight, caught the blow, and the thin cane cut through the flimsy muslin. Another cut followed, tearing it still more, until after about half a dozen the frail stuff tore right away and hung down in ribbons. I warmed to the work and deftly cut more away at each stroke. The stuff, thin as it was, acted as some sort of protection – though not much – to her body, for as it fell away only slight weals showed on the skin. When the garment was in tatters, I took hold of it and ripped it right away so that she stood there quite naked, save for a little yoke of muslin left round her shoulders.

During this part of her punishment involuntary cries came from her, but not a tear. Her lips were set and she was evidently determined not to break down if she could help it.

I laid the cane aside and took up a birch. 'Now,' I said, 'your bottom shall get what you evidently expected just now. Now tell me, will you disobey me again, will you, will you? . . . Answer me when I speak to you! answer me, I say.' Sharp biting cuts punctuated each question, but not a word came from the set lips of the determined girl. I was provoked at her obstinacy and rained blow after blow on the slim legs and cheeks. She bore every attack in silence; her flesh flinched each time the stinging twigs fell but otherwise she displayed no feeling.

Muriel had followed the punishment so far in silence, but now seeing that the girl remained stubborn, she roused herself painfully and said, 'I'll make her speak, let *me* help.' She got out of bed and, taking the wire birch in her hand, came haltingly towards her victim. 'Bend her right down, Cecil, lower than that, lower still – that's better.' I bent the stiff body right down – it might have been made of stone, so unyielding was it – until the head was as low as the knees. The skin of the bottom was consequently stretched quite tight. Muriel separated the legs so that they formed a triangle. 'Now young lady, I'll teach you to spy on me.' The little wire birch hissed in the air and fell. A shriek of agony came from Ethel. She fell forward in spite of my hold on her.

'Oh, Uncle, don't let her . . . I'm sorry . . . you whip me if you like, but not her . . . oh, oh, oh!' The birch fell again and again, each point piercing the skin and drawing blood. 'Oh, Uncle, tell her to stop, I'll never disobey you again, oh, Auntie, I'm sorry, oh don't don't!'

She writhed and twisted on the floor. I signed to Muriel to stop, for the blood was trickling down the white thighs. 'That will do for now,' I said. 'Now Ethel, every morning for a week you are to come to your aunt and Juliette and myself and say, "I'm sorry I was disobedient and spied on you; please whip me as I deserve." Do you understand? Every morning before you dress – now go to Gladys and ask her to wash you and put you to bed and I'll bring you up your dinner.'

Ethel rose to her feet, white and tear-stained, and silently went out of the room. I followed her after a minute or two and found her being soothed by Gladys. When she saw me she looked imploringly at me. 'I'm truly sorry, Uncle,' she said, 'I am really. But need I be whipped by Auntie? Won't it do if you whip me?'

'Certainly not,' I answered. 'You spied on your aunt, and must pay for it.'

'But *three* whippings every morning!'

'I told you, you'd be sorry,' said Gladys, 'but you wouldn't listen.'

Those morning whippings of Ethel came to be for me one of the best parts of the day. To be awakened out of sleep by the touch of a light hand and to hear a small voice say, 'Uncle, I'm here; I'm sorry I spied on you, please whip me as I deserve,' helped an already rampant member to sit up and take an interest in things.

The first one or two mornings Muriel and Juliette were rather severe and the poor little bottom was still sore from the wounds of the wire birch. She came sobbing into my room and threw herself into my arms, begging to be let off. But that I would not do altogether. I contented myself, however, with roughly tracing the word 'spy' – one letter a morning – on the front of her thighs and stomach with the riding whip. The lash just flicked little red weals on the skin and six cuts were enough for each letter.

On the fourth morning Muriel and Juliette had evidently let her off more lightly, for there were no tears. I accordingly had less scruples as regards my share. I made her lie on her back on the bed and hold each leg by the ankle as wide apart and as far back as possible. In this position she showed absolutely all there was to show. I took a few twigs from a birch and flicked her everywhere, making the ends of the twigs curl wickedly into every secret cranny. At first she seemed to like it rather, for she only squealed now and then and laughed wickedly up at me from between her knees. I remembered it was punishment, not pleasure, and gave her several hard cuts with the twigs all up and down the inside of her thighs and between the cheeks of her bottom, until the twigs broke off short. These blows changed her tune and she soon cried out for mercy.

The next morning I tied her by the ankles to the bed-rail, so that her head was on the ground, and encircled her thighs and flanks with a whip. She had come in rather cheekily, evidently thinking her punishment was nearly over or ought to be, and I thought it as well to show her that some atonement was still required. She certainly presented rather a pathetic figure tied up as she was with her nightdress fallen down over her head and her slim white body and legs at the mercy of the lash. In her position she could not move much, only writhe and twist her body, while, from underneath the nightdress, shrill cries greeted each cut. When I released her she crept sobbing to my feet, imploring forgiveness and mercy. I could not help pitying her, but the fierce joy of inflicting pain and the lust for torture were stronger than the pity, and I had just self-control enough that morning not to inflict some really serious harm on the girl.

She must have seen the struggle going on in me, for she flung her arms round me and said, 'You don't hate me, Uncle, do you, although you hurt me so? . . . I don't mind your hurting me, but don't hate me, for I love you.' I kissed her passionately and sent her away to her own room.

On the last day of her seven, she came to my room very merry and bright. 'Have you been to Aunt and Juliette?' I asked. 'Oh yes, but they were in bed together; they were far too busy with each other to attend to me. They just smacked me once each and told me to come to you. Uncle, I'm quite ready for you.' She cheekily pulled up her nightdress and bent down.

'Say what you have to say.'

'I'm sorry I spied on you; please whip me as I deserve.' She rattled the words off quickly with a 'don't care' air.

'Right!' I said. 'I will.' I got out of bed, laid her across my knee and brought my hand smartly down on the tempting bottom. I did not spare her this morning and soon the skin began to grow pink and my palm began to smart. I got up and reached for my hairbrush, then, making her bend forward, I stood on one side of her and smacked her, pretty severely, with the back of it. My pyjamas were loose and began to fall, exposing John Thomas ready, as usual in the early morning, for anything. Ethel looked up at me and, seeing that I wasn't really angry, began to play with him and fondle him. I continued smacking her, until she began to protest. 'Ooh, you do hurt this morning. I suppose it's because it's the last time. Ooh!'

An idea struck me. 'Yes, we'll finish well,' I said. 'Wait a moment,' and I got on the bed, lying on my back. 'Now get on top of me . . . no, the other way . . . that's right, now across me and kiss me nicely.' She took John Thomas in her mouth and her eager lips and tongue began caressing it.

'I haven't done this, for a long time, I *do* love it! Ooh! that's lovely! . . . I don't like *that* though.' Her little bottom just came within reach of my tongue, and as I caressed her tiny slit, I continued to smack the rounded cheeks with the brush. The blows fell harder as I felt the goal approaching and she began to wriggle. I held her still with my left hand, and when John Thomas at last responded to the caresses of her tongue, I rained a rapid shower of blows all over the rounded surface. Her own nature answered mine at the same moment and I drank greedily of her young fresh love.

She fell full-length on top of me, her knees giving way under the stress of her passion, and she sucked and drew all my strength from me with her eager lips and tongue, while her slender fingers squeezed and fondled the balls that hung down between my thighs. I have seldom given such a copious flow as she drew from me that morning. Yet she scarcely seemed satisfied. Even when John Thomas had yielded all he had to give for the moment she still continued to suck, until he dwindled and softened and she reluctantly let him go.

❧ 12 ❧

A Sacrifice to Aphrodite Pandemos

That certain morning's adventure had quite different effects on Muriel and Juliette. The latter soon recovered her normal spirits and seemed to forget and ignore what had happened. With Muriel it was quite different. Hers was a far more highly strung and sensitive nature, and for some days she seemed entirely overwhelmed. I waited anxiously, with daily enquiries and investigations, for reassuring proof that no lasting results and awkward and serious consequences had resulted from the adventure. Within a few days I was satisfied in the case of Juliette, but there was still a week to wait before I could know the truth about Muriel.

During this time her moods were very varying. At first she seemed quite stunned and apathetic. She roused herself the first morning or two to wreak some vengeance on Ethel, but even that failed to interest her after a few days, as I have told. Then she became very hysterical and irritable. At first I tried kindness and solicitude, but she grew so peevish and ill-tempered that I lost patience and threatened her with harsh measures if she did not control her temper better. She did not take much notice, so after some recrimination on her part I felt that kindness and forbearance were no good and gave her a sound whipping. She took it passively, saying nothing when it was finished. There was a look of fixed intention in her eye which I could not fathom, but though she said nothing the pain evidently had some effect, for the rest of the day she was far less sulky and irritable.

At last I went to her in bed one morning and found her in tears. 'What's the matter?' I asked. She wouldn't answer, and growing tired of repeating my question without any reply, I pulled the clothes down, intending to thrash an answer out of her. Then I saw that her nightdress was stained with blood, and I realised that I need have no further fear of any consequences. My anger disappeared at once. I gave a sigh of relief. 'Thank God!' I said.

She looked at me. 'Why?' she asked.

'That,' I answered, pointing to the stains.

She suddenly flared out at me. 'Yes, that's just like you men, selfish and cruel. The pleasure of the moment – that's all you want. But I want more. I want something to remind me of him always.'

'What on earth are you talking about?' I said. 'What do you mean? You surely don't mean to say that you want a baby!'

'Yes, I do, I want *his* baby.'

'His! whose?' She was silent. 'Tell me, what do you mean? Are you suddenly gone mad or what?'

'I want a baby by *him*.' She moaned, and burst into a passion of tears. I was silent, for the situation was beyond me. After she had sobbed out her passion to some extent and had grown calmer she turned to me imploringly. 'Oh, Cecil, I want him so, I must have him, do let me have him again. You may beat me, torture me anyway you like, but only let me feel him mix with me again!'

'What on earth are you talking about?'

'That man, that day,' she stammered.

I was thunderstruck. Then I turned on her in a rage. 'How dare you? Are you mad? You want to prostitute yourself to that yokel, that clod! You deserve – I don't know what you deserve – !'

'I know, I know, Cecil dear; but I can't help it – it makes me terribly ashamed but I can't resist it. Oh, let me go to him, let me have him. Then I will be your slave again as long as you like. I'll do anything, I'll suffer anything, only let me have just this one satisfaction.' She writhed all over the bed clutching at me with imploring hands, exposing all her body as she twisted about in her passion. The sight of her lascivious gestures fired me and I took her in my arms and regardless of her condition possessed her. She welcomed me gladly and with utter abandon.

When I had finished she murmured, 'That was kind and sweet of you, dear; but – don't be angry – it's *him* I want. I love *you*, but I want *him* – oh, do let me have him, do let me, just once – only once – I promise you it shall be only once.'

I could not understand her. 'I must think,' I said. 'If I *do* let you, you will probably have to pay severely for it.'

'I'll pay any price you like,' she answered.

I went away and sought Juliette, and told her the facts of the case. 'What do you advise?' I asked her.

'I'm not altogether surprised,' she answered. 'I know she was absolutely carried beyond herself by the second man. We've talked about that morning, and she as good as told me what she has said to you.'

'Well, what's to be done?'

'It's up to you,' she answered. 'If you don't mind her being had by other men, and I rather think you liked it the other morning, why not let her have her way?' I was silent for a moment.

'If I do, it must be done in my own way,' I said, 'and I don't know if the gentleman will consent to that. I must be there to see.'

'Let us all be there,' said Juliette; 'that may perhaps cure Muriel of her infatuation, when she discovers that we all know about it.'

I thought about it for a day or two, and when Muriel was herself again, I decided to go over and sound out her bucolic Adonis. I took with me the skirt that had been lent to cover her nakedness, as a cloak for my visit. When I arrived at the cottage, I found the woman at home. She grinned at me when she opened the door.

'Good-morning, I've brought your skirt back.'

'Oh, have 'ee,' she laughed. 'I never thought to see 'ee again, young man. My man's been in a terrible way about your lot. 'E turned coward after you'd gone, like all men, and was afeared for what might 'appen. I told 'im 'e needn't worry, but 'e's terrible anxious.'

'You tell him from me, he needn't be afraid; where's the other man? I want to speak to him.'

'Which one? There were three of 'em.'

'Oh, the other one that . . . that . . . ' I did not know how to finish the sentence.

' 'Im that vucked your missus after my man 'ad vinished, d'ye mean?' she said boldly. I nodded. 'Oh 'e's at work. 'E'll be 'ome soon, if so you'ld like to wait. Come inside, young man, I'm all alone.' Her meaning was unmistakable, but I had no desire or intention whatever of gratifying her desire. 'You baint afeared of me, sure-lie! Come along I won't eat 'ee.' What might have happened I don't know, but at that moment the two girls who had started the fracas the other morning appeared in the distance. 'Dang the brats!' said the woman. 'They be always in the way when they baint wanted.' Then, as she saw my eye following their young figures as they ran towards us, she went on, 'Ah! that's what'ud suit you, eh young man, I don't doubt, but they be too young as yet. That'd mean 'sizes business for 'ee.'

I laughed nervously, for I didn't know I had betrayed myself by my expression. 'No, no, you're quite wrong; I wasn't thinking of that at all. I was only thinking of the other morning when they got smacked. I suppose they often get smacked, don't they?'

'Not more than is good for them, the young limbs! Look 'ere mister,' she said suddenly, 'be you that sort of young man? . . . Oh I know,' she went on, as I kept silence, 'I was in service in my young days and I know what my master and missus used to do. I saw the marks on your missus's bottom, t'other morning, be you one o' they whipping chaps?' I smiled. 'I thought as much,' she nodded. 'Now look 'ere, would 'ee like me to smack 'em before 'ee now? What would 'ee do if I did, eh?' she smiled up at me provokingly. She really was not a bad-looking woman, in spite of the coarsening effects of her hard life.

'You had better wait and see,' I said. The girls had stopped when they saw me talking to their mother. They evidently had recognised me and were approaching nervously.

'Where 'ave you been, Sally and Mary?' shouted their mother. 'I told 'ee to 'urry back, come 'ere and say good-marnin' to the gentleman, and then tell me where you've been. I lay I'll pay your bottoms well, you lazy little varmints.' They came nervously towards me and bobbed a curtsey. 'Sally, go and fetch me the strap.' The child gave her mother a frightened look but obeyed. The other girl made a start as if to run away. 'Catch 'old of 'er mister, don't 'ee let 'er go.' I did as I was asked, and Sally returned with the strap. In a minute she was under her mother's arm with her skirts turned up – she wore no drawers – and a hail of blows from the strap was descending on her bottom and thighs. From the cries and the plunging of her legs, she was catching it pretty hot. 'Now Mary, it be your turn. Pull 'er clothes up, will 'ee, mister, and I'll tan 'er young 'ide.' I was not slow in doing what I was asked, as may be guessed. I bent the young body down so that the head was between my thighs and then uncovered all the back and legs. Down came the strap right across the plump cheeks, leaving a broad red mark. Mary was about a year younger than her sister but plumper and more developed. Again and again fell the strap, and from between my legs came muffled cries for mercy. The strap evidently was a most effective though noisy weapon. 'There, that'll teach 'ee to loiter, you young devils,' at last said the mother, 'now be off and tell Ben a gentleman wants to see 'im, 'e's working over at varmer Thorpe's. That be two mile away,' she added to me, as the girls ran painfully away. 'Now, young man, what be 'ee agoin' to pay me for the show?'

I looked at her. In spite of her general untidiness and blowsiness, she was a fine figure of a woman. In her younger days she must have been decidedly handsome in a coarse way. Now she looked like some savage queen, holding the lash.

'What do you want?' I asked. An unaccountable longing to be mastered by her came over me.

'You know what I want, young man, come inside.'

'I don't know that I'll give it to you,' I said, 'unless you take it.' I looked meaningly at her and at the strap. 'Oh,' she said, 'be it like that with you? It'll be old master and missus over again. I've listened at the door. I know.'

Before I quite knew what was happening, she had seized hold of my trousers – I was wearing loose flannels and a sash – and had ripped the fly open. They fell round my knees. She then gripped me round the waist and drew me down across her knee. I yielded in a strange kind of fascinated stupor. To this day I cannot account for it or explain it. I am not by nature a masochist – my whole tendency being entirely the other way – but at that moment I had only one desire, one passion – to submit my body to the domination of this woman. She was not slow to take advantage of my mood. She dragged the trousers well down, placed one leg over mine imprisoning me between her knees, raised my shirt well over my back, and then . . . oh, the murderous agony of that first blow. It entirely cured me of any masochistic desire at that moment. But it was too late. Her left hand pressed firmly on my back, her knees gripped my legs, I was powerless. Blow followed blow, now here, now there. The pain was awful. I set my teeth and tried to bear it, but it was no good. The tears and cries would come. 'Ah!' she hissed, 'I'll teach 'ee, you miserable worm; won't vuck me, won't 'ee, what good be 'ee, what did 'ee marry me for? I'll teach 'ee.' I gathered that she was quoting her old mistress.

At last my cries and sobs became more unrestrained, my prayers for mercy more agonised. I promised anything.

'Let me go,' I prayed, 'I'll do anything, oh let me go.' I joined words of love and endearments with my prayers, I tried to find her sex with my hands, pulling up her skirt and stroking her thigh. At last she released me and I stood tottering and shaking before her. She looked at me triumphantly and then without a word took hold of my member and, making me kneel before her as she sat in the chair, opened her legs and drew me right inside her. The paroxysm came almost at once, but she would not let me go. She held me close to her, and by fierce caresses of my balls and every method she could think of, she succeeded in forcing a second erection and drained me again of my manhood.

❧ 13 ☙

Saeva *Venus*

I went home in a kind of ecstasy. My whole nature was in a turmoil. I was smarting terribly from the strap and was longing for, not exactly revenge – that was not the word I wanted – but for others to share my pain. I must whip someone, somehow; whip them as I had been whipped – cruelly, mercilessly. Who should it be? Muriel? Juliette? Ethel or Gladys? Gladys? Yes, the idea appealed to me most strongly. I was fondest of her; she loved me, I knew; she was the gentlest of the four; she gave me, too, least cause for punishment. Yet if I could find or make an excuse, I would whip her, whip her till the blood ran. I had told the woman to send Ben to me late that afternoon and so had some hours free. When I got to the cottage I found Muriel in bed, asleep. Juliette and Ethel were out. Gladys was waiting for me. How my heart leapt at the sight of her! How I longed to torture and cut that slender fragile body. She came running towards me. 'Oh, Uncle, wherever have you been? I've been waiting for you for such a long time. What have you been doing?'

'What's that to do with you?' I answered roughly. 'How dare you be inquisitive about my doings!'

She started at my rough tone. 'Uncle,' she gasped, 'what's the matter? I didn't mean . . . '

'I'll show you what's the matter, I'll teach you to question me.'

'But, Uncle.'

'Go upstairs at once. I'll follow you.' She went in without a word, as white as a sheet. I went to my room, chose a cane, and followed her. She trembled when she saw what was in my hand. 'Take your drawers off,' I said.

'But, Uncle, why! I haven't done anything.'

'Do as I tell you, take those drawers off and lie across the bed. I'll teach you to be inquisitive.'

'But, Uncle, oh don't,' as the cane fell across her shoulders.

'Will you take them off!' Her nervous fingers fumbled for the buttons and at last the flimsy muslin fell round her ankles. '*Now*, turn your skirts up and lie across the bed.' She obeyed bewildered. 'Now take that, and that, and that. How dare you ask questions as to where I've been, and what I've been doing? Just because I've been kind to you and not punished you as I've punished your sister, you think you can presume. But I'll teach you. There, there, there and there.'

'Oh, Uncle, don't, oh, don't! What have I done? I'm sorry, oh, Uncle, please . . . '

'Take that hand away, take it away – there then,' and the cane fell on the wrist, extorting a howl of anguish from the poor girl. Blue livid weals began to appear all over the rounded cheeks and thighs. The cries turned to dull moans. The soft bruised flesh flinched at each blow of the cane. My passion began to abate and after some half a dozen cruel cuts I threw the cane – all bent by this time – into a corner and lifted the quivering body into my arms. Her eyes were half-closed, her cheeks were deathly pale, I thought at first that she had fainted, but when she felt my arms around her drawing her to me, she opened her eyes and murmured, 'Oh, Uncle, why! What did I do? What made you whip me like that?'

I sat on the bed and tried to take her in my arms. She could not bear to sit on my knee. She was too bruised, but she lay half on her face on top of me, her arms clinging round my neck. The tears streamed down her cheeks, and her whole body shook with emotion.

We stayed like that for some time and at last she grew quieter and I recovered my sanity. I gently disengaged myself and set about repairing the ravages of my rage. As I tenderly anointed her bruised flesh with the emollient cream I always had handy, she again murmured her oft-repeated question – 'Oh, Uncle, why! What had I done?'

When she had grown still calmer, and was lying on her side, I told her what had happened. As I expected, she did not wholly understand. Her chief feeling was one of rage and jealousy against the woman. 'The beast, the beast!' she kept on murmuring. 'Oh, I wish I had her here. Oh, Uncle, darling, everyone has you but me; Uncle darling, take me, take me, I want you, I want you . . . see!' She rolled over on her back, wincing as she rested on her bruised flesh, and opening her legs as wide as she possibly could, she parted with her fingers the lips of her virgin pussy. Had it not been that I had been drained dry already, I probably should have taken her at her word; as it was, I bent down, and fastening my lips to those delicious pouting ones, I sucked and drained her until I felt she had no more to give. She sighed and moaned in ecstasy, her hands caressing my hair. At last, as I drew away, she murmured, 'Ah, that was heaven, but I'm sure the real thing must be better still. Oh, Uncle, did you really let that beastly woman whip you! I'd kill her if I had the chance. Did she hurt you much? Let me see.' She drew me towards her and, unbuttoning my trousers, found John Thomas, who was doing his best to stand and weeping at his failure. She kissed him all over and then, lifting my shirt, gazed at my bruised behind. 'Oh, poor, poor bottom,' she said. 'I don't wonder you wanted to hurt someone else. And you hurt me because you love me best, was that it?' I nodded. 'Yes, I think I understand, and I'm glad; oh, poor, poor bottom.' She bent down and covered both cheeks with soft tender kisses, letting her soft smooth tongue caress the bruises gently. Then, giving each cheek the daintiest of little pats, she smiled up at me. 'There, I've smacked you too; now, cover it up and let's go out and find the others.'

As we went along, I told her all about Muriel's sudden and strange passion for the man who had violated her, and how I had discussed the matter with Juliette, and how we had agreed that she should have a chance to gratify her passion *but* in our presence. 'She does not know that part of it,' I said. 'In fact, I haven't told her at all that I have agreed to it, but I think I shall. Ben (that's his name, from what the woman tells me) is coming to see me this afternoon, and if he consents to what I shall propose, your aunt will be sacrificed to Aphrodite Pandemos in the presence of all of us.'

She was silent for a moment or two, and then she said, as if thinking aloud, 'Yes – I think I see – but how can she want anyone else when she has *you*, Uncle? Oh, I wish . . . Uncle, will there be any whipping of *him*? If there is, let me do it – it will be nearly as good as whipping that awful woman . . . Will you let me? Do, please.'

'I don't quite know what will happen,' I answered. 'Neither of them as yet knows that anything is going to take place; but if I see my chance, you shall have what you want.' She kissed me fondly and we went on to find the others.

After tea that afternoon I was smoking a cigarette outside the cottage, and I saw a figure coming across the beach; I thought I recognised the man and went to meet him. It was Ben. ' 'Evenin', zur,' he said. 'My sister told me as 'ow you wanted me.' He looked rather nervous, as if not quite certain as to what was in store for him, but in spite of his rather hang-dog air, he was still a fine figure of a man – a perfectly developed animal, healthy and full-blooded.

'Yes,' I said, 'it's like this; your exploit of the other morning has had rather unexpected results. Instead of being enraged with you, as she might have been, the lady whom you possessed has conceived a great desire for you and has asked me to get you to see her again. Now I am willing that she should gratify her desire on one condition – that you do exactly as I order; that you – in a word – place yourself entirely at my disposal, submitting to everything I say.'

'I don't understand 'ee, zur,' he said. 'You zay the lady wants me? Aye, I thought as much. I zaid at the time 'er loved me. Aye and I love 'er, but what do 'ee want?'

'I want *this*,' I said. 'She's my mistress, and if I lend her to you, you must both be utterly in my power, at the moment, to do what I like with. I am quite sure of her, I know – but you – well, I must be sure that I have you utterly in subjection if I let you enjoy her, will you consent to this?'

'I don't follow your meanin', zur; be I to vuck 'er? or what do 'ee want I to do?'

'Yes, certainly, but other things may happen while that is going on. Now, will you consent to have your arms tied together while you are enjoying her; or will you swear to me that you will submit to any treatment while your pleasure lasts? . . . Oh, you needn't be afraid . . . nothing serious will happen, but I want to know where I am before I start.'

He scratched his head. 'I don't rightly know, zur,' he said, 'what exactly you're at; but I do want 'er again, that's a fact, and if so be I be so fortunate as to 'ave 'er, I don't much mind what happens. My sister, she've told me that you're a gentleman who likes fancy tricks, and she've told me arl about this marnin' ' – he added with a grin – 'so I be ready for anything of that kind if it's that you want.'

'Right,' I said. 'Wait just a moment, and I'll get things ready.' I went into the cottage, leaving him outside. I found Muriel still in bed. 'Muriel,' I said, 'I've found you the man you want; he's outside; shall I bring him up?'

She could hardly believe her ears. 'Oh, Cecil, you darling,' she said, 'do you really mean it?'

'Yes, he's waiting.'

'Oh, let me get ready for him; oh, how wonderful you are!' She jumped out of bed and searched in the chest of drawers for a clean nightdress. Seeing the scent spray on the dressing-table, she sprayed herself all over, and began brushing her hair. It might have been a devotee preparing for religious mysteries rather than a lustful woman preparing for her lover. I smiled grimly and went down to muster the others. Juliette and Gladys, of course, knew what to expect, but Ethel was quite ignorant. I warned the other two in whispers to keep her well in hand, and then went out to find Ben. I took him up to my own room and suggested that he had better take his clothes off.

He did so slowly and shyly. 'Where be I to go, zur,' he said. 'I do 'ope as no one will zee me naked like this!'

'This way,' I said when he had stripped, leading the way to Muriel's room. I had lighted all the candles in the room. Muriel was lying in a most seductive nightdress. When he crossed to the bed I called to the others. They came quietly up the stairs, and just as Ben, after kissing Muriel, was preparing to get on top of her, they all filed into the room. He stopped as if thunderstruck. His rampant engine wilted; an acute fit of nervousness seized him. He looked round.

'What be this, zur?' he asked. 'I bain't used to making love in public.'

'You said you would submit to me; it's either this way or no way at all. Put out your hands.' He did so mechanically, and before he knew what had happened, I had slipped the handcuffs which I knew so well from personal experience on his wrists.

'Now,' I said, pulling back the bedclothes and raising Muriel's nightdress so that her legs and stomach were exposed to the gaze of all of us, 'there's the woman who wants you, there's the woman whom you want. Take her and enjoy her.'

The sudden shock and surprise had for the moment taken away his erection. He looked at me and then at himself. 'I can't do nothin' like this, zur; I be nervous.'

'Gladys,' I said, 'you wanted the chance this afternoon, go to that case and fetch a birch.' I gave her the key and she quickly took out a birch. 'Now, see if you can make our friend fit for his duty.' The yokel looked all eyes at this. It was evidently beyond his comprehension. 'Now, Gladys, give him some keen cuts across his bottom. You needn't be afraid of hurting him. His skin's pretty tough, I expect.' Gladys needed no second order. She brought the birch heavily down across the brawny buttocks.

Ben jumped away. 'What's the meaning of this?' he shouted. 'I baint agoin' to be whipped.'

'You keep quiet, my man,' I said. 'Curl it between his thighs, Gladys; now touch him up in front a little, that's better.' I saw his old man twitch nervously and, bending forward, took hold of it. It answered to my touch and rose magnificently. 'Now,' I said, 'do your duty.' I helped him on top of Muriel and placed his member at the entrance of what it desired. Then I ventured to undo the handcuffs and left him free. I stopped Gladys's blows for the moment and watched the scene on the bed. Muriel, past all sense of shame in the gratification of her desire, was receiving her lover with open body, arms, and legs. Her loins met his impassioned thrusts, and when I saw that they were nearing the end of their course, I signed to Gladys to continue her chastisement. Her blows fell quicker and quicker, as the man's loins worked in ever-quickening plunges; at last I saw that the supreme moment was coming, and seizing the birch from Gladys's hands, I rained a shower of carefully directed blows on the heaving buttocks and thighs. He took no notice of my attack, but like a high-couraged racehorse under the whip over the last furlong, put forth all his efforts for the final sprint, and at last, clutching Muriel's bottom with his hands, he first dragged her to him and then collapsed on top of her, having spent his final energy. I stopped my assault and looked round. Gladys was on the other side of the bed to me, watching the scene with wide eyes of fascinated wonder. On my side of the room Juliette and Ethel had at first been standing silent spectators, but now I saw that the scene had proved too much for them; Juliette had sunk on a chair and drawn Ethel on top of her. She had pulled her skirts up and Ethel's busy fingers were eagerly probing her most secret recesses. The two bodies on the bed were closely entwined in the abyss of passion.

When I thought that they had lain long enough like this, I touched Ben on the shoulder. 'Well,' I said, 'did you enjoy it?' He got up rather sheepishly, and grinned. 'That be a new game to I,' he said, 'to be whipped while one be vucking, but it baint bad.'

'Well, next time,' I said, 'it will be the other way about; you lie on the bed, and when you're ready she shall get on top of you.'

'I be ready now,' he answered, and sure enough I saw that his old man was rising again. 'I'll soon make 'ee fit,' he went on, rubbing himself vigorously. Muriel up to this time had appeared not to notice our presence in the room. We had all come in after Ben had appeared naked before her and had just begun to mount her. Possibly her desire for him had overcome any latent shame or modesty, and she had decided to take all she could get just as she could get it. But now, when she saw Ben lying beside her on his back encouraging his engine for a second attack, and when I went to her and told her to get on top of him, she whispered to me, 'I didn't bargain for this, Cecil; I didn't mean that the girls should see this.'

'You do as you are told,' I said. 'Get on top of him; you wanted him, you've got him; you ought to be very grateful that you have him at all.'

She made no further protest but got up and knelt across the massive body. Then, taking his affair in her hand, she placed it just between her lips and, slowly sinking down, impaled herself on it. When I saw her well fitted, 'Now,' I said, 'you two, make her work.' I gave Gladys back the birch and fetched another for Ethel, and the two, standing on either side of the bed, rained blow after blow on the plunging thighs and loins. Muriel heaved and plunged as the blows fell; groans and sighs of mingled passion and pain came from her lips. Ben clutched her round the waist with his brawny arms and moved with her plunges. At last, however, the supine position irked him, unused to it as he evidently was, and he twisted round, and, without disengaging his body, managed to work himself on top of her. The blows of the birches now fell on him, instead of on Muriel, but he paid no attention to them. His buttocks heaved and fell. His thighs opened and closed and at last after a few vicious mighty thrusts he collapsed motionless on Muriel's body.

In the meantime Juliette and I had not been idle. Beginning with mutual caresses, I at last pulled her on to my lap with her back to me, and finding her eager inviting pussy, I slipped my old man into it, and while watching the contest on the bed, I rode her on my knee until I gave and took from her all I wanted.

This last bout had practically finished Muriel. When I got Ben off her, she lay just as she was, not caring to hide her nakedness at all. The lips of her pussy were still wide open and a small stream of viscous matter trickled from between them. Ben had evidently given her all she could hold. I motioned him to follow me out of the room, and led him back to where his clothes were. As he was dressing, I said to him, 'Well, are you satisfied?'

'I've had a rare proper good time, zur,' he said, 'but what beats me is why you let me do it. You've got a vine wench there, and yet you let me 'ave 'er.'

I smiled. 'No, my friend, I don't suppose you *do* understand; but I'll tell you this much. She's mine, as you say, to do just what I like with, and if I choose to give her to anyone that's my affair. If I choose to give her to a *dog*, I will, she daren't refuse. If on the other hand, I refuse to allow her any single thing she may want, still she has to submit – but there, it beats you, as you say, so we won't say any more about it. Good-night to you, and keep your mouth shut. It may happen again if you hold your tongue – so mum's the word.'

'You may trust me, zur,' he replied. 'I'm mum as an oyster. Good-night and thank 'ee.'

❧ 14 ❧

The Roman Dinner

The orgy described in the last chapter was the last of any note which we had at Croyde. Muriel, the next day, seemed somewhat – I won't say exactly ashamed – but at any rate subdued. *Post coitum omne animal triste est*, says the Roman philosopher, and it was certainly true in her case. She was uniformly affectionate and dutiful to me, but she seemed to have lost her interest in the holiday. The weather, too, became bad, and altogether we came to the conclusion that London in the wet was better than the country. We accordingly packed up and departed from Croyde, arriving at the little house in South Molton Street late one evening at the end of August.

There was still a fortnight or so of holidays left to the girls and we decided that theatres and Earl's Court should take the place of sea-bathing and picnics. For more intimate pleasures Muriel's boudoir was far better fitted than the cottage. I seized the opportunity too of running down to Oxford to take my degree and, after paying the necessary fees to the university and my scout, was duly received as a Bachelor of Arts.

I came back to town and determined to have one glorious evening before the girls went back to school. I had told Muriel something of my idea and she agreed gladly. I doubt if she had known the details she would have consented so readily. But that is by the way. In a word I determined to revive a night under the Roman Empire, as far as modern conditions would allow. Muriel's bathroom lent itself to this especially. As I have said, it was a hobby of her husband's, being more like a plunge in a Turkish bath than an ordinary bathroom. It was all of marble about four feet deep with steps leading down into it. It was heated by a hypocaust and about twelve feet long. One could swim or float in it in comfort.

The bath was to begin the evening. Afterwards there was to be a feast. For this Muriel's boudoir was admirably adapted. The divan, or couch, made a very good substitute for a triclinium and a table was the only other necessary piece of furniture. I ordered in a special cold supper from Benoist's, so that it could be kept handy and served without outside help. I chose dishes as nearly Roman as were palatable – flamingos' tongues were of course unobtainable. The wine was the only thing modern. A visit to Clarkson's for costumes, etc., was the only other preparation.

The entertainment began in the bath. I made all the girls strip naked and did the same myself. Then, while Muriel, Juliette and Gladys stood naked on one side of the bath as attendants, I revived with Ethel the Spintria, as described by Suetonius. In strict accuracy Ethel ought to have been a boy, but in the circumstances I decided that that was not a very important point and might be waived; though later in the evening I did my best to remedy that, as will be seen.

For those who don't know their Suetonius and his description of Tiberius's life at Capri I will describe the Spintria. I floated on my back in the bath and Ethel swam slowly between my legs, caressing all my private parts with her hands and mouth until the natural result happened. When that was over we came out of the water and the three girls received us with towels and soap and massaged us thoroughly. Then they sprayed us with scent, dressed us in Roman clothes, crowned us with garlands, and led us to the feast. Before we took our seats, I did my best to turn Ethel into a boy. Amid much giggling from the others, I produced an exquisite model of a boy's private parts, modelled in what actors call 'nose paste', and stuck it on to Ethel's mons Veneris with spirit gum (a friendly assistant at Clarkson's proved very useful to me for this); so we arrived at the table. Now a small difficulty arose. Muriel had evidently expected that she would (so to speak) be the guest of the evening. But I quickly undeceived her. 'During the first part,' I said, 'the parts are cast as follows: I am the patrician who gives the feast; Ethel is a favourite slave; you and Gladys are attendants, and Juliette shall be a tumbler to entertain us. When the feast is over we shall all enjoy ourselves as we like.'

'But, have I to wait on Ethel?' pouted Muriel.

'Certainly,' I said, 'and you may as well dress for the part now; it was to come later, when the wine had taken effect, but you may as well begin. I decide to be waited on by birds this evening.

'What do you mean?'

'This,' I said, producing some peacock feathers which I had obtained. 'Peacocks shall wait on me – bend down and let me fix them.'

'But where, how, I don't understand.'

I took hold of her, bent her forward and began to place the quill of a peacock feather where the peacock carries his.

She sprang away – 'I won't, I won't, it's beastly.'

'Oh is it?' I said. 'Remember, you're in Rome now, or rather Pompeii.' I seized hold of her and with a quick twist flung her to the ground; then, seizing a whip which was handy, as one would always have been in ancient Rome, I thrashed her naked body until she begged for mercy. 'Now,' said I, 'will you wear the feathers or not?'

'Oh yes, yes,' she sobbed. I raised her to her feet and again bent her forward, found the tiny hole I was looking for and inserted three lovely feathers. 'Now, Gladys, for you.' Gladys came towards me trembling. 'Don't hurt me, Uncle, please, oh! oh! oh! don't push it up too hard; oh, it makes me feel so ashamed.' The sight of these two naked girls walking about with the peacock's feathers sticking out behind excited my passions tremendously, I turned to Juliette. 'Now Juliette, when I call for you, you are to dance and tumble as I showed you yesterday.' I had rehearsed her in her part and shown her reproductions of some Pompeian frescoes.

So we sat or rather lay down to dinner – Ethel and I side by side on the couch, served by Muriel and Gladys. Ethel, in the shortest of *gitons* with her hair tied in a Grecian fillet, looked lovely, and as course followed course and the wine went to my head, my hand wandered under her tunic and disclosed the false sex of a boy with which I had endowed her. She seemed very proud of it and spread her legs, showing it off. Muriel, however, did not like it, any more than she liked the peacock decoration. She showed her disgust or at any rate disdain in every movement. I waited my opportunity. At last in serving me with wine she spilled some over my arm as I held the glass. I sprang up at once – the scene by this time had entered into my brain, and I was for the moment a Roman noble, haughty and passionate. I seized her by the wrists and dragged her to the wall, where cords were hanging from a hook. I tied her wrists to these and, calling for rods, I thrashed her bare back and thighs until she begged for mercy. Then, returning to the table, I clapped my hands for Juliette. She appeared swaying her hips and undulating her belly in a most lascivious manner. She was naturally very supple and she managed very successfully to reproduce the indecent contortions and postures described by the later Roman poets and depicted on the hems and mural decorations of the period.

Ethel watched eagerly – her naturally naughty mind welcomed this indecent display. I plied her with wine and, drinking heavily myself, began to toy with her, probing underneath the artificial sex which I had given her. Her nature responded at once. I turned her over on her side with her back to me and without shame or hesitation began to play in real earnest the part of a Roman noble with his favourite slave. She was surprised at this method of attack. 'You're in the wrong place, Uncle,' she said.

'Not at all,' I panted in answer, as I pushed my way, 'this is Ancient Rome and you're a boy, not a girl.'

'Oh don't, you're hurting me.'

'Bear it just a little more, it won't hurt then . . . that's better . . . *now*.' I began to work; the years slipped away, I was back again at school in my fourth year – I was back in Ancient Rome – I was no longer Cecil Prendergast but a patrician of the Empire; Nero the Artist was Emperor. I held Ethel close to me in my ecstasy, one finger penetrated right into her burning pussy, and as I felt her warm life flooding my hand, I poured all my strength into her. The feast was now over. I summoned my attendants to me on the couch and, disengaging myself from Ethel, I made them bathe us both with scented water. Then the wine went round again and under its influence and my caresses Muriel began to forget that she had not up till then played the chief part in the entertainment. Every form of lascivious enjoyment was indulged in, until at last morning broke on five naked bodies interlaced in one confused medley on the couch.

Two days later the girls went back to school, looking forward to the Christmas holidays, when we were all to meet again. Gladys's last words to me were, 'I shall be patient, Uncle; but I mean you to have me properly then. I shan't be able to wait any longer, I know. You will do everything to me then, won't you? Promise me.'

I promised her I would see what could be done, and when the train left the station, Muriel, Juliette, and I went back to South Molton Street to devise fresh pleasures among ourselves and to wait for the Christmas holidays.

Wordsworth Classic Erotica

❧ ❧

WORDSWORTH DISTRIBUTION

Great Britain and Ireland
Wordsworth Editions Limited
Cumberland House, Crib Street
Ware, Hertfordshire SG12 9ET
Telephone 01920 465 167
Fax 01920 462 267

USA, Canada and Mexico
Universal Sales & Marketing Inc
230 Fifth Avenue, Suite 1212
New York, NY 10001, USA
Telephone 212-481-3500
Fax 212-481-3534

Italy
Magis Books SRL
Via Raffaello 31c
Zona ind Mancasale
42100 Reggio Emilia, Italy
Telephone 0522-920999
Fax 0522-920666

**Germany, Austria and
Switzerland**
Swan Buch-Marketing GmbH
Goldscheuerstrabe 16
D-7640 Kehl am Rhein, Germany

Portugal
International Publishing
Services Limited
Rua da Cruz da Carreira, 4B
1100 Lisboa
Telephone 01-570051
Fax 01-352-2066

Spain
Ribera Libros S L
Poligono Martiartu, Calle 1, no 6
48480 Arrigorriaga, Vizcaya
Tel. 34-4-671-3607 (Almacen)
Tel. 34-4-441-8787 (Libreria)
Fax 34-4-671-3608 (Almacen)
Fax 34-4-4418029 (Libreria)